the
people look
like flowers
at last

also by **CHARLES BUKOWSKI**

available from **ECCO**

The Days Run Away Like Wild Horses Over the Hills (1969)

Post Office (1971)

Mockingbird Wish Me Luck (1972)

South of No North (1973)

Burning in Water, Drowning in Flame: Selected Poems 1955–1973 (1974)

Factotum (1975)

Love Is a Dog from Hell (1977)

Women (1978)

You Kissed Lilly (1978)

play the piano drunk like a percussion instrument until the fingers
   begin to bleed a bit (1979)

Shakespeare Never Did This (1979)

Dangling in the Tournefortia (1981)

Ham on Rye (1982)

Bring Me Your Love (1983)

Hot Water Music (1983)

There's No Business (1984)

War All the Time: Poems 1981–1984 (1984)

You Get So Alone at Times That It Just Makes Sense (1986)

The Movie: "Barfly" (1987)

The Roominghouse Madrigals: Early Selected Poems 1946–1966 (1988)

Hollywood (1989)

the people look like flowers at last

new poems

CHARLES BUKOWSKI

EDITED BY JOHN MARTIN

ecco
An Imprint of HarperCollinsPublishers

HarperCollins books may be purchased for educational, business, or sales
promotional use. For information, please write: Special Markets Department,
HarperCollins Publishers, 10 East 53rd Street, New York, NY 10022.

FIRST EDITION

Designed by Cassandra J. Pappas

Library of Congress Cataloging-in-Publication Data is available upon request.

ISBN: 978-0-06-057707-0
ISBN-10: 0-06-057707-X

07   08   09   10   11   WBC/QBF   10   9   8   7   6   5   4   3   2   1

contents

three

four

one

the heart roars like a lion

at what they've done to us.

for they had things to say

the canaries were there, and the lemon tree
and the old woman with warts;
and I was there, a child
and I touched the piano keys
as they talked—
but not too loudly
for they had things to say,
the three of them;
and I watched them cover the canaries at night
with flour sacks:
"so they can sleep, my dear."

I played the piano quietly
one note at a time,
the canaries under their sacks,
and there were pepper trees,
pepper trees brushing the roof like rain
and hanging outside the windows
like green rain,
and they talked, the three of them
sitting in a warm night's semicircle,
and the keys were black and white
and responded to my fingers
like the locked-in magic
of a waiting, grown-up world;
and now they're gone, the three of them
and I am old:
pirate feet have trod
the clean-thatched floors
of my soul,
and the canaries sing no more.

evening class, 20 years later

the hungry tug of too late;
webs of needles,
the same trees are here;
and grass grown on grass
but the faces now are young
and as you walk across the campus thinking
"memory is a poor excuse for the present"
the legs want to let the body fall as
old images cling to you like mollusks
and the girls now gone who once
claimed your substance
hang like broken shades
across the windows of your mind;

—at one time here
everything was mine—

now young lions claim the territory
and look out casually
over loose paws
and decide
mercifully
to let this poor game crawl by. he, of course,
no match for the young lionesses,
or the Spring in the early sky.

at one time here—
once—

I enter a room and stand against a wall
and hear my name read, and
no, it is not the same:

my old professor looked like a walrus
as he spit my name out
into the spittoon of the world
and I said, HERE! while
feeling the sun run down
thru the hair of my head
like wires feeding life into life:
white rain, sea wild;

but this new one whispers my name (and it is dark);
and like a claw reaching down into some pit of me,
surrounded by walls like tombs I answer meekly,
here,
and he moves on to another name.
I am older than he
and certainly not as fortunate
as the lionesses curl at his feet and purr delightedly,
and one gray old cat
twists its neck
and asks me: have you been here before?

yes, yes, yes, yes
I have
been here
before.

the snow of Italy

over my radio now
comes the sound of a truly mad organ,
I can see some monk
drunk in a cellar
mind gone or found,
talking to God in a different way;
I see candles and this man has a red beard
as God has a red beard;
it is snowing, it is Italy, it is cold
and the bread is hard
and there is no butter,
only wine
wine in purple bottles
with giraffe necks,
and now the organ rises, again,
he violates it,
he plays it like a madman,
there is blood and spit in his beard,
he wants to laugh but there isn't time,
the sun is going out,
then his fingers slow,
now there is exhaustion and the dream,
yes, even holiness,
man going to man,
to the mountain, the elephant, the star,
and a candle falls
but continues to burn upon its side,
a wax puddle shining in the eyes
of my red monk,
there is moss on the walls
and the stain of thought and failure and
waiting,

then again the music comes like hungry tigers,
and he laughs,
it is a child's laugh, an idiot's laugh,
laughing at nothing,
the only laugh that understands,
he holds the keys down
like stopping everything
and the room blooms with madness,
and then he stops, stops,
and sits, the candles burning,
one up, one down,
the snow of Italy is all that's left,
it is over: the essence and the pattern.
I watch as
he pinches out the candles with his fingers,
wincing near the outer edge of each eye
and the room is dark
as everything has always been.

near a plate glass window

dogs and angels are not
very far apart.
I often go to this little place
to eat
about 2:30 in the afternoon
because all the people who eat
there are completely sane,
glad to be simply alive and
eating their food
near a plate glass window
which welcomes the sun
but doesn't let the cars and
the sidewalks come inside.

across the street is a Chinese
nudie bar
already open at 2:30 in the
afternoon.
it is painted an
inane and helpless
blue.

we are allowed as many free
coffees as we can drink
and we all sit and quietly drink
the strong black coffee.

it is good to be sitting some place
in public at 2:30 in the afternoon
without getting the flesh ripped from
your bones.

nobody bothers us.
we bother nobody.

angels and dogs are not
very far apart
at 2:30 in the afternoon.

I have my favorite table
by the window
and after I have finished
I stack the plates, saucers,
the cup, the silverware, etc.
neatly
in one easy pile—
my offering to the
elderly waitress—
food and time
untorn,
and that bastard sun
out there
working good
all up and
down.

beef tongue

I hadn't eaten for a couple of days
and I had mentioned that several times
and I was up at this poet's place
where a tiny woman took care of him.
he was a big bearded ox with a brain twice as large as the
world, and we'd been up all night
listening to tapes, talking, smoking, swallowing pills.
his woman had gone to bed hours ago.
it was 10 a.m.
and the sunlight came on in not caring that we hadn't slept
and the next thing I knew
he was coming out of the kitchen
saying, "hey, Chinaski! LOOK!"
I couldn't see clearly—
at first it looked like a yellow boot filled with water
then it looked like a fish without a head
and then it looked like an elephant's cock,
and then he brought it closer:
"beef tongue! beef tongue!"
he held it out at arm's length
right in my face:
"BEEF TONGUE! BEEF TONGUE!"
and it *was*, and I never imagined a steer's tongue was that
fat and long,
it was a rape,
they had gone deep into the creature's throat
and hacked it out, and here it was now:
"BEEF TONGUE!"
and it was yellow and pink
and
it was gagging all by itself

just another reasonable and sensible atrocity
committed by intelligent men.
I was not an intelligent man. I
made it to the sink and began to
heave.
stupid, of course, stupid, it was only dead meat,
no feeling now, the pain long since run out of the bottom of the
world
but I continued to vomit, finished, cleaned up the sink
and walked back
in. "sorry," I said.
"it's o.k., I forgot about your stomach."
then he walked the tongue back into the kitchen
and then came out and we talked of this and that
and in about ten minutes
I heard the water boiling and I smelled the tongue cooking
in that bubbling water without mouth or eye
or name, it was a huge tongue going around and around
under that lid
and stinking
becoming cooked tongue
becoming most delicious and flavored
but since he was an agreeable fellow
I asked him please to turn it off.

it was a cold morning and as I shivered in the doorway
as I got ready to leave
the new air was good
I could feel the legs the heart the lungs
beginning to envision another chance.

we talked about a book of poems he was helping me
edit, then I said "goodbye, keep in
touch," and we didn't shake hands, a thing neither of us
liked to do
and I went up the path and out to my car and started the
engine and as I warmed it up I imagined him moving back into the
kitchen behind that mass of black beard,
those blue diamond eyes shining out of
all that *black* hair
those intelligent happy blue diamond eyes
knowing everything (almost), and then
turning the flame on again
the water beginning to shift and simmer
the tongue moving around in there
once again.

and I, stupid in my machine, turned away from the
curb, let it roll through the yellow morning,
down around the curves and dips,
all that green growing nicely along the side
of the road.

well,
thank Christ he hadn't invited me to stay to
dinner. when I got home I thumbed through some
Renoir, Pissarro and Diaz
prints. then I ate a hard-boiled
egg.

the 1930s

places to hunt
places to hide are
getting harder to find, and pet
canaries and goldfish too, did you notice
that?
I remember when pool halls were pool halls
not just tables in
bars;
and I remember when neighborhood women
used to cook pots of beef stew for their
unemployed husbands
when their bellies were sick with
fear;
and I remember when kids used to watch the rain
for hours and
would fight to the end over a pet
rat; and
I remember when the boxers were all Jewish and Irish
and never gave you a
bad fight; and when the biplanes flew so low you
could see the pilot's face and goggles;
and when one ice cream bar in ten had a free coupon in-
side; and when for 3 cents you could buy enough candy
to make you sick
or last a whole
afternoon; and when the people in the neighborhood raised
chickens in their backyards; and when we'd stuff a 5 cent
toy auto full of
candle wax to make it last
forever; and when we built our own kites and scooters;
and I remember
when our parents fought

(you could hear them for blocks)
and they fought for hours, screaming blood-death curses
and the cops never
came.

places to hunt and places to hide,
they're just not around
anymore. I remember when
each 4th lot was vacant and overgrown, and the landlord
only got his rent
when you had
it, and each day was clear and good and each moment was
full of promise.

people as flowers

such singing's going on in the
streets—
the people look like flowers
at last

the police have turned in their
badges
the army has shredded its uniforms and
weapons. there isn't any need for
jails or newspapers or madhouses or
locks on the doors.

a woman rushes through my door.
TAKE ME! LOVE ME!
she screams.

she's as beautiful as a cigar
after a steak dinner. I
take her.

but after she leaves
I feel odd
I lock the door
go to the desk and take the pistol
from the drawer. it has its own sense of
love.
LOVE! LOVE! LOVE! the crowd sings in the
streets.

I fire through the window
glass cutting my face and
arms. I get a 12-year-old boy

an old man with a beard
and a lovely young girl something like a
lilac.

the crowd stops singing to
look at me.
I stand in the broken window
the blood on my
face.

"this," I yell at them, "is in defense of the
poverty of self and in defense of the freedom
not to love!"

"leave him alone," somebody says,
"he is insane, he has lived the bad life for
too long."

I walk into the kitchen
sit down and pour a
glass of whiskey.

I decide that the only definition of
Truth (which changes)
is that it is that thing or act or
belief which the crowd
rejects.

there is a pounding at my
door. it is the same woman again.
she is as beautiful as finding a
fat green frog in the
garden.

I have 2 bullets left and
use them
both.

nothing in the air but
clouds. nothing in the air but
rain. each man's life too short to
find meaning and
all the books almost a
waste.

I sit and listen to them
singing
I sit and listen to
them.

acceptance

16 years old
during the Depression
I'd come home
and my possessions—
shorts, shirts, stockings,
suitcase and many pages
of short stories—
would be thrown out on the
front lawn and about the
street.

my mother would be
waiting behind a tree:
"Henry, Henry, don't
go in . . . he'll
kill you, he's read
your stories.
please take
this . . . and
find yourself a room."

but since it worried him
that I might not
finish high school
I'd go back
again.

one evening he walked in
holding
one of my short stories
(which I had never shown
him)

and he said, "this is
a great short story!"
and I said, "o.k.,"
and he handed it back to me
and I read it:
and it was a story about
a rich man
who'd had a terrible fight with
his wife and had
gone out into the night
for a cup of coffee
and had sat and studied
the waitress and the spoons
and forks and the
salt and pepper shakers
and the neon sign
in the window
and wondered about it all,
and then he went
to his stable
to see and touch his
favorite horse
who then
for no reason
kicked him in the head
and killed him.

somehow
the story had some
meaning for him
though
when I wrote it

I had no idea
what I was
writing about.

so I told him,
"o.k., old man, you can
have it."

and he took it
and walked out
and closed the door and
I guess that's
as close
as we ever got.

life at the P.O.

I huddle in front of this maze
of little wooden boxes
poking in small cards and letters
addressed to nonexistent
lives
while the whole town celebrates
and fucks in the street and sings
with the birds.
I stand under a small electric light
and send messages to a dead Garcia,
and I am old enough to die
(I have always been old enough to die)
as I stand before this wooden maze
and feed its voiceless hunger;
this is my job, my rent, my whore, my shoes,
the leeching of the color from my eyes;
master, damn you, you've found me,
my mouth puckered,
my hands shriveled against my
red-spotted sunless chest;
the street is so hard, at least
give me the rest I have paid a life for,
and when the Hawk comes
I will meet him halfway,
we will embrace where the wallpaper is torn
where the rain came in.
now I stand before wood and numbers,
I stand before a graveyard of eyes and mouths
of heads hollowed out for shadows,
and shadows enter
like mice and look out at me.

I poke in cards and letters with secret numbers as
agents cut the wires and test my heartbeat,
listen for sanity
or cheer or love, and finding none,
satisfied, they leave;
flick, flick, flick, I stand before the wooden maze
and my soul faints
and beyond the maze is a window
with sounds, grass, walking, towers, dogs,
but here I stand and here I stay,
sending cards noted with my own demise;
and I am sick with caring: go away, everything,
and send fire.

the minute

"I am always fighting for the next
minute," I tell my wife.
then she begins to tell me
how mistaken I am.
wives have a way of not
believing what their husbands
tell them.

the minute is a very sacred
thing.
I have fought for each one since my
childhood.
I continue to fight for each one.
I have never been bored or
at a loss what to do next.
even when I do nothing,
I am utilizing my time.

why people must go to
amusement parks or movies
or sit in front of tv sets
or work crossword puzzles
or go to picnics
or visit relatives
or travel
or do most of the things
they do
is beyond me.
they mutilate minutes,
hours,
days,
lifetimes.

they have no idea of how
precious is a
minute.

I fight to realize the essence
of my time.
this doesn't mean that
I can't relax
and take an hour off
but it must be
my choosing.

to fight for each minute is to
fight for what is possible within
yourself,
so that your life and your death
will not be like
theirs.

be not like them
and you will
survive.

minute by
minute.

too near the slaughterhouse

I live too near the slaughterhouse.
what do you expect? silver blood
like Chatterton's? the dankness of my hours
allows no practiced foresight.
I hear the branches snap and break
like ravens in a quarrel,
and see my mother in her coffin
not moving
quietly not moving
as I light a cigarette
or drink a glass of water
or do anything ignominious.
what do you want?
that I should feel
deceived?

(the green of the weeds in
the sun
is all we have
it's all we really have.)

I say let the monkeys dance,
let the monkeys dance
in the light of God.
I live too near the
slaughterhouse
and am ill
with thriving.

a future congressman

in the men's room at the
track
this boy of about
7 or 8 years old
came out of a stall
and the man
waiting for him
(probably his
father)
asked,
"what did you do with the
racing program?
I gave it to you
to keep."
"no," said the boy,
"I ain't seen it! I don't
have it!"

they walked off and
I went into the stall
because it was the only one
available
and there
in the toilet
was the
program.

I tried to flush
the program
away
but it just swam
sluggishly about

and
remained.

I got out of
there and found
another
empty stall.

that boy was ready
for his life to come.
he would undoubtedly
be highly successful,
the lying little
prick.

stranger in a strange city

I had just arrived
in another strange city
and I had left my room and
found myself walking along
on what must have been
a main thoroughfare where
the autos ran back and
forth with what seemed to be
a definite
purpose.
that busy boulevard seemed to
stretch away endless
before me and
appeared to run
straight off to the edge of
the earth,
and then
after walking awhile
I realized
that I was
lost, that
I had forgotten the name
of the street my
room was on
or
where it was.

there was nothing back
in that room
but a week's paid
rent
plus a battered

suitcase
full of my old clothes
but it was
everything I
possessed
so I began searching
the side streets
looking for
my room
and I soon became
frightened, a
numb terror like a fatal
illness
spreading through me
as
I kept walking
up and down unfamiliar
streets
until my mind
said to me:
you're crazy, that's
all, you should
give up and turn
yourself in
somewhere.

but I just kept walking.

it had been a
long afternoon and now
it was slipping
into evening.

my feet ached
in my cheap
shoes.

then it grew
dark, now it was night,
but I just kept
walking.

it felt as if
I had walked
up and down through
the same streets
over and over.

then finally
I recognized my
building!
and I ran
up the steps
and up the interior
stairway to
the 2nd floor
and my room was still
there and I
opened the door,
closed it behind me,
and was
safely inside.

there was the
suitcase

on the floor,
still full of my
old clothing.

I heard a man
laugh
in one of the other
rooms and I suddenly
felt a lot
better.

I took off my shoes,
shirt, pants,
sat down on the edge
of the bed and
rolled a
cigarette.
then I leaned back against
the pillow and
smoked.

I was 20 years old
and had 14 dollars
in my wallet.

then I remembered
my wine bottle.
I pulled it out
from under the
bed, uncapped it
and had a good
hit.

I decided that I
wasn't crazy.

I picked a newspaper up
off the floor
and turned to the
HELP WANTED section:

dishwasher, shipping
clerk, stock boy,
night watchman . . .

I threw the paper down
on the floor.
I'd look for a
job
day after
tomorrow.

then I put the
cigarette out
satisfied
and went to
sleep.

just another wino

the kid was 20, had been on the road
5 or 6 years and he sat on the couch
drinking my beer, his name was Red,
and he talked about the road:
"these 2 guys were trying to treat me
nice, keep me quiet, because I'd seen them kill a
guy."
"kill a guy? how?"
"with a rock."
"what for?"
"he had his wallet, a good
wallet, and 7 dollars. he was a wino. he was
drunk and they hit him with the rock,
knocked out his brains."
"you saw it?"
"I saw it. the next time the train stopped
they dumped him out, they dumped him in some
high grass. then the train started up
again."
I gave the kid another beer.

"when the police find those guys in rags, no
identification, wine-faced, they say 'just another wino,'
they don't even follow up, they just
forget it."
we talked most of the night
about the road. I told him a few stories of my
own. then I went to bed. he slept on the
couch. I went into the bedroom with the woman and
kid. slept.

when I got up to piss in the morning
Red was sitting in a chair
reading yesterday's paper.
"I gotta go," he said, "I can't sleep
anymore, but I had a good night, some good
talk. thanks."
"me too, Red. easy now."
"sure."
then he was out the door and down the street,
gone.

back in the bedroom she asked, "is Red gone?"
"yeah."
"where'd he go?"
"I don't know. Texas. Hell. Boston. anywhere."
the little girl woke
up: "I wanna bottle!"
"can you get her a bottle? you're up."
"sure."

I went into the kitchen and mixed some
milk. and everywhere things were working out there,
cruel and not cruel, spiders and bums
and soldiers and gamblers and madmen and
factotums and fags and firemen, like that,
and I went back in and handed the girl the bottle
got back into bed
and listened to the kid sucking on the thing—
suck suck suck,
and soon we'd have our own
breakfast.

it is not much

I suppose like others
I have come through fire and sword,
love gone wrong,
head-on crashes, drunk at sea,
and I have listened to the simple sound of water running
in tubs
and wished to drown
but simply couldn't bear the others
carrying my body down three flights of stairs
to the round mouths of curious biddies;
the psyche has been burned
and left us senseless,
the world has been darker than lights-out
in a closet full of hungry bats,
and the whiskey and wine entered our veins
when blood was too weak to carry on;
and it will happen to others,
and our few good times will be rare
because we have a critical sense
and are not easy to fool with laughter;
small gnats crawl our screen
but we see through
to a wasted landscape
and let them have their moment;
we only asked for leopards to guard
our thinning dreams.
I once lay in a
white hospital
for the dying and the dying
self, where some god pissed a rain of
reason to make things grow
only to die, where on my knees

I prayed for LIGHT,
I prayed for l*i*g*h*t,
and praying
crawled like a blind slug into the
web
where threads of wind stuck against my mind
and I died of pity
for Man, for myself,
on a cross without nails,
watching in fear as
the pig belches in his sty, farts,
blinks and eats.

the bull

I did not know
        that the Mexicans
                did this:
                      the bull
had been brave
        and now
                they dragged him
                      dead
around the ring
        by his
            tail,
                a brave bull
                    dead,
but not just any bull,
            this was a special
                    bull,
and to me
        a special
            lesson learned . . .
                and although Brahms
stole his First from Beethoven's
                9th
            and although
the bull
        was dead,
                his head and his horns and
his intestines dead,
        he had been better than
                Brahms,
                    as good as
            Beethoven,

and

     as we walked out

            the sound and meaning

                of him

kept crawling up my arms

and although people jostled me and

stepped on my toes

the bull burned within me

            my candle of

               light;

dragged by his tail

         he had nothing to do with anything

          now having escaped it all,

and down through the long tunnel, surrounded by

elbows and feet and eyes, I prayed for Tijuana

and for the dead bull

        and man

          and me,

              the blue kissing waters

enjoying the knot of pain,

        and I clenched my hands

              deep within my

pockets, seized darkness

        and moved on.

the people, no

startling! such determination in the
dull and uninspired
and the copyists.
they never lose the fierce gratitude
for their uneventfulness,
nor do they forget to laugh
at the wit of slugs;
as a study in diluted senses
they'd make any pharaoh
cough up his beans;
in music they prefer the monotony of
dripping faucets;
in love and sex they prefer each other
and therefore compound the
problem;
the energy with which they propel their
uselessness
(without any self-doubt)
toward worthless goals
is as magnificent as
cow shit.
they produce novels, children, death,
freeways, cities, wars, wealth, poverty, politicians
and total areas of grandiose waste;
it's as if the whole world is wrapped in dirty
bandages.

it's best to take walks late at
night.
it's best to do your business only on
Mondays and
Tuesdays.

it's best to sit in a small room
with the shades down
and
wait.

the strongest men are the fewest
and the strongest women die alone
too.

you might as well kiss your ass goodbye

I finally met him. he sat in an old robe
and bitched for 5 hours.
"look," he said, "don't trust Krause,
Krause will rob you. he owes me 10,000 dollars
and there's no way I can get it out
of him. a real bastard."

"Sir," I said, "when you wrote that first novel,
it was so humorous, the truth is always so funny,
you know, the way people act, like blind mechanical things,
killing without reason, marvelous how you got it all
down."

an old woman came in and set a pot of tea in front of
him. "they smashed my motorcycle, stole my manuscripts,
cleaned me out. they would have killed me but I wasn't
here. they called me a fascist, claimed I sold the plans
to the Maginot Line to the Krauts. now where the hell would I ever
get the plans to the Maginot
Line?"

he poured his tea. lifted the cup. it was too hot
or something. he spit it out on the rug, some of it
on my shoes and pants.

"Sir," I asked, "that first novel, did you really eat your own
flesh as a young writer? were you that
hungry? by god, that was some novel, I'll never
forget it!"

"Martha!" he called. "Martha!"

the old woman came in.

"you forgot the lemon and sugar, you old hag!"

the old woman ran out
for the lemon and sugar.

"the government claims I owe them 70,000 dollars! they don't bother
    Krause. the son-of-
a-bitch rides around in a Cadillac and owns a twelve
acre estate. don't ever trust Krause. he's a bloodsucker. he's sucked
the bodies and talents of at least 3 dozen writers dry. he's like a giant
spider, a tarantula!"

"Krause has never asked me for anything . . ."

"if he does, you might as well kiss your ass
goodbye!"

Martha ran in with the lemon and sugar.

"you damned washed-up whore! I oughta whip your ass!"

"Sir," I said, "you're looked up to
as one of the strongest writers since 1900."

"don't trust Krause! a bloodsucker!"

he bitched for 5 hours. and I listened. then his head fell back,
across the top of his rocker, and I saw that
famous hawk profile. then he began
to snore.

he was just an old man in an old
bathrobe.

I stood up. Martha came in.

"I'm glad I had a chance to meet him,"
I told her.

"I try to remember he was once a great writer,"
she told me.

"he's still kind of humorous,"
I told her.

"I don't think so," she said,
"you see, I'm his
wife."

"goodnight," I
said.

"goodnight," she
replied.

purple glow

I see the high-heeled
shoes and a dried white rose
lying on the bar
like a clenched
fist.
whiskey makes the heart beat faster
but it sure doesn't help the
mind and isn't it funny how you can ache just
from the deadly drone of
existence?

I see this
nudie dancer running along the top of
the bar
shaking what she thinks is
magic
with all those faces staring
up from overpriced
drinks.

and me? being there? no shit,
I really didn't care about
her but I love the pulse of
the loud flat music thumping
in the purple glow, some-
thing about it all: I hardly
ever felt better.

I watch her, the purple
doll so
sad so cheap so
sad, you would never want to

bed down with her or even hear her
speak, yet in that drunken place
you would
like to hand your heart to her
and say
touch it
but then
give it back.

she dances so fiercely now in
the purple glow,

purple does something strange to me:
there was a night
30 years ago
I was drunk, true, and there was
a purple Christ in a glass box
outside a little church and I
smashed the glass, I broke
the glass, and then I reached in and touched
Christ but
He was only a dummy and I heard the
sirens then and started
running.

well, my mind has never been the same
since and the typing helps but you can't
type all the time, so the nudie dancer now
breaks what heart I have left and I
don't know why but I start giving money
to everybody in the bar, I give a five to this
guy, a ten to that, I think maybe it might

wake them to the wisdom
of it all
but they don't even say
"thanks," they just think I'm a
fool.

the manager comes up and tells me
I'm 86'd, I hand him a
twenty, he takes
it.

two friends
have been sitting at a back
table, they help me up and out of the
bar.
I think the situation is very
funny but they are
angry:

where's your car?

where's your fucking
car?

I say, I
dunno.

too fucking bad, they
say and
leave me sitting alone on an
apartment house
step.

I light up and smoke a cigarette,
then get up and begin the long
walk, a walk I know will
entail at least a couple of
hours
to find my car (past experience)
but I know that when I
find it, the rush of
happiness will be
all I need
and that I will then be able to
begin my life all over
again.

one thousand dollars

all of my knowledge about horse racing
told me that this was a sure bet.
I bet one thousand to win.
the horse had post one
at 6 furlongs.

the bell rang and they came
out of the gate.

my horse turned left
ran through the fence
fell down and
died
right there
at 7/5.

when I tell people this story
they don't say
anything.

sometimes there's nothing to say
about
death.

grip the dark

I sit here
drunk now
listening to the
same symphonies
that gave me
the will to go on
when I was 22.

40 years later
they and I are not quite so
magical.

you should have
seen me then
so
lean
no
gut
I was
a gaunt string of a
man:
blazing, strong,
insane.

say one wrong
word
to me
and I'd crack you right
there.

I didn't want to be
bothered with

anything or
anyone.

I seemed to be
always on my way to some
cell
after being booked for
doing things
on or off the
avenue.

I sit here
drunk now.
I am
a series of
small victories
and large defeats
and I am as
amazed
as any other
that
I have gotten
from there to
here
without committing murder
or being
murdered;
without
having ended up in the
madhouse.

as I drink alone
again tonight
my soul despite all the past
agony
thanks all the gods
who were not
there
for me
then.

the dwarf with a punch

this is many years later
and I still can't figure it out
but it was in New York
and New York has its own rules and
anyhow, I am sitting around in one of those
places
with many round tables
with their tough and terrible knights;
me, I don't feel so good, as usual,
neither tough nor terrible,
just rotten,
and I am sitting with some woman
with some kind of hood over her head,
she is half crazy
but that doesn't matter.
she has a name, Fay,
I think it was,
and we have been drinking, going from place to
place, and we went in there,
and it seemed terribly
lively
because there was a dwarf about 3
feet tall
and the dwarf was walking around
drunk
and he'd stop at a table
and look at a man
and say,
"well, what YOU got to say?"
and then the dwarf would crush him one in the mouth,
only the dwarf had very good hands and
one hell of a punch.

then everybody would laugh and the dwarf would
go to the bar
for another drink.
"keep him away from me, Fay!" I told her.
"uh? whatzat? what? who?"
"keep him away from me!"
"what? waz? away?"
the dwarf unloaded on another guy
and everybody laughed,
even I laughed. that dwarf could punch.
he had a lot of
practice.
he danced to the bar
doing a little soft shoe
then he noticed a sailor
very blond and young and
scared.
the kid pissed in his pants
and smiled at the
dwarf.
the dwarf chopped him a
good one;
his next smile was a
bit bloody.
then the dwarf put another on his chin
knocking the sailor over
backward in his
chair, out
cold.
k.o.! all hail the
champion!
then the dwarf saw

me. the man at the table in
back.
"keep him away from me, Fay!"
I said.
"lez have another drink!" she said.
(she had a full drink in front of her.)
he came up to me
in all 3 feet of his
glory.
"well, what YOU got to say?"
I didn't answer. I didn't have anything to say
that he would understand.
"nothing, hah?"
I nodded. it came. I felt my chair rock, then
settle again on its legs. shots of red and yellow and
blue light followed, then laughter.
sitting there
I swung back.
his poor 3 feet slid along the floor like a
rag doll
and then they were down on me
it seemed like a dozen men
(but it might have been 3 or 4)
and I caught some more
good ones.
then I was thrown outside,
I got up
and found a hanky
and tried to stop
the worst of the blood
and Fay was there,

"you coward, you hit that little
man!"
I walked down the street
but she was right there with me
and we went into the next place
and I looked around
and seeing that everyone was more than
4 feet tall,
I ordered 2 more
drinks.

the elephants of Vietnam

first they used to, he told me,
gun and bomb the elephants,
you could hear their screams over all the other sounds;
but you flew high to bomb the people,
you never saw it,
just a little flash from way up
but with the elephants
you could watch it happen
and hear how they screamed;
I'd tell my buddies, listen, you guys
stop that,
but they just laughed
as the elephants scattered
throwing up their trunks (if they weren't blown off)
opening their mouths
wide and
kicking their dumb clumsy legs
as blood ran out of big holes in their bellies.

then we'd fly back,
mission completed.
we'd get everything:
convoys, dumps, bridges, people, elephants and
all the rest.

he told me later, I
felt bad about the
elephants.

breakfast

waking up on those mornings in the drunk tank,
busted lower lip, loose teeth, brains swimming in
a cacophony not yours, with
all those strange others swathed in rags, noisy
now in their mad sleep, with nothing for
company but a stopped-up toilet,
a cold hard floor
and somebody else's
law.

and there was always one early voice, a loud voice:
"BREAKFAST!"

you usually didn't want it
but if you did
before you could gather your thoughts
and scramble to your feet
the cell door was slammed
shut.

now each morning it's like a slow contented
dream, I find my slippers, put them on,
do the bathroom bit, then walk down the
stairway in a swirl of furry bodies, I am
the feeder, the god, I clean the cat bowls, open
the cans and talk to them and they get excited and
make their anxious sounds.
I put the bowls down as each cat moves to
its own bowl, then I refill the water dish
and watch all five of them eating
peacefully.

I walk back up the stairway to the bedroom
where my wife is still asleep, I crawl beneath
the sheets with her, place my back to the sun
and am soon asleep again.
you have to die a few times before you can really
live.

inverted love song

I could scream down 90 mountains
to less than dust
if only one living human had eyes in the head
and heart in the body,
but there is no chance,
my god,
no chance.
rat with rat dog with dog hog with hog,
play the piano drunk
listen to the drunk piano,
realize the myth of mercy
stand still
as even a child's voice snarls
and we have not been fooled,
it was only that we wanted to believe.

Salty Dogs

got to the track early to study the odds and here's
this man coming by
dusting seats. he keeps at his work, dusting, most
probably glad to have his simple job.
I'm one of those who doesn't think there is much difference
between an atomic scientist and a man who cleans the seats
except for the luck of the draw—
parents with enough money to point you safely toward a more
generous life.

"how's it going?" I asked him as he dusted by.

"o.k., how about you?" he asked.

"I do all right with the horses. it's with the women I lose."

he laughed. "yeah. a man has two or three bad experiences,
it really sets him back."

"I don't mind two or three," I told him, "I mind
eleven or twelve."

"man, you must know something by now. who do you like in the
first?"

I told him that Salty Dog was reading 4-to-1 and should
finish one-two. (45 minutes later it did.) but it wasn't 45
minutes later yet. the man went on dusting and I thought of all my
rotten jobs and how glad I was to have them. for a
while. then it was a matter of quitting or getting fired.
both felt good.

it's when you live with one woman for more than two
years you know what's bound to happen only you don't know
exactly why. it's not in the chart. it's in past performance,
not in the chart.

my friend, dusting the seats, he didn't know exactly why either.

I walked over for a coffee. the slim girl behind the
counter was a brunette with a tiny blue flower in her hair,
nice eyes, nice smile. I paid for my coffee.

"good luck," she said.

"you too," I said.

I took the coffee to my seat, the wind came up from the west,
I took a sip and waited for the action, thinking of
many things, too many things. the scene dissolved into grass and
trees and the dirt track and I remembered dirty shades in
dirty rooming houses flapping back and forth in a light wind,
and I thought about dirty troops plundering some new village,
and about my old girlfriends unhappy again with their new men.

I sat and drank my coffee and waited for the first
race.

brainless eyes

in the bitter morning
high roses grow
and the frogs celebrate
victory.

in the empty balloon of night
nothing grows;
the night
gnaws and belches
and victory is celebrated only
by indecent ladies
with spread legs
and brainless eyes.

at noon,
say at noon,
something happens
finally.

the signal changes
the traffic moves through.

life itself is not the miracle.
that pain should be so constant,
that's the miracle—
that hammer of the thing
when you can't even scream or weep
and it sits all over you
looking into your eyes
eating your flesh.

morning night and noon
the traffic moves through
and the murder and treachery
of friends and lovers
and all the people
move through you.

pain is the joy of knowing
the unkindest truth
that arrives without
warning.

life is being alone
death is being alone.

even the fools weep

morning night and noon.

unbelievable

I've been going to the track for
decades
but I saw something new
today.
2 horses threw their riders.
usually when a horse throws
his or her rider
he (or she) continues to run
in the same direction as
the other horses.
but
this time
both horses turned
and began to run in the
opposite direction,
in other words,
toward the oncoming
field.
it was a 5/8ths mile
track
and they were
approaching one another
pretty fast.
the announcer warned
the riders
and as they came
around the last curve
and into the stretch
here came the other
2 horses right at
them.

there was no screaming.
there was a dead
silence.
you could hear the hooves
pounding the dirt.

then one horse swung
wide
and went outside the
field.
the other headed straight
into it
and passed right through
between the other
horses.

the other horses reached
the wire.

mine had won.

but the judges held an
inquiry and it was
declared
no contest.

I didn't give a
damn.

I kept seeing that horse
rushing at the field
and passing right through,
untouched.

a miracle.

war and peace

to experience
real agony
is
something
hard
to write about,
impossible
to understand
while it
grips you;
you're
frightened
out of
your
wits,
can't sit
still,
move
or even
go
decently
insane.

and then
when your
composure
finally
returns
and you are
able to
evaluate
the

experience
it's almost as
if it
had happened
to
somebody
else

because
look at
you
now:

calm
detached

say

cleaning your
fingernails

looking through
a
drawer
for
stamps

applying
polish
to your
shoes

or
paying the
electric
bill.

life is
and is not
a
gentle
bore.

the harder you try

the waste of words
continues with a stunning
persistence
as the waiter runs by carrying the loaded
tray
for all the wise white boys who laugh at
us.
no matter. no matter,
as long as your shoes are tied and
nobody is walking too close
behind.
just being able to scratch yourself and
be nonchalant is victory
enough.
those constipated minds that seek
larger meaning
will be dispatched with the other
garbage.
back off.
if there is light
it will find
you.

beware women grown

old

who were never

anything but

young.

all the little girls

it was up in northern California
and he stood in the pulpit
and he had been reading for some time
he had been reading many poems about
Mother Nature and the inherent goodness
of man.

he believed that everything was
all right with the world.
and you couldn't blame him:
he was a tenured professor who had never
been in jail or in a whorehouse;
who had never had his used car die
on the freeway; who
had never needed more than
three drinks during his wildest
evening;
who had never been rolled, flogged or
mugged;
who had never been bitten by a dog;
who got regular gracious letters from Gary
Snyder, and whose face was
kindly, unmarked and
tender. finally,
his wife had never betrayed him,
nor had his luck.

he said, "I'm just going to read
three more poems and then I'm going
to step down from here and let
Chinaski read."

"oh no," said all the
little girls in their pink and blue
and white and orange and lavender
dresses. "oh no,
read some more, read some
more!"

he read one more poem and then he said,
"this is the last poem that
I will read."

"oh no," said all the little
girls in their red and green see-
through dresses. "oh no," said
all the little girls in their tight blue
jeans with little sewn hearts on them.
"oh no," said all the little girls,
"please read
more poems!"

but he was as good as his word.
he got the poem out and he got down and
vanished somewhere. as I got up to read
the little girls wiggled in
their seats and one of them hissed and
some of them made interesting remarks to me
which I will use in a poem at some later date
because this particular goddamned poem
has to end somewhere.

anyway, it was two or three weeks later
when I got this letter from the poet William
saying that he *did* enjoy my reading.
he was a true gentleman.
I was in bed with a
three-day hangover. I lost the envelope
but I took the letter and folded it
into one of those paper airplanes
I had learned to make in grammar
school. it sailed around the room
and landed between an old Racing Form
and a pair of well-worn shorts.

we have not corresponded since.

no more of those young men

my first husband, Retzel, she said,
flew gliders. he had only one hand.
he never went down on me even once.
he wants to meet you, he lives in
Redondo Beach.

Redondo Beach, I said, Redondo Beach.

my next husband,
Craft, took pills and played the piano all day.
then he had to have one of his fingers operated on.
a wart. he was cruel to me. he knows now
how cruel he was to me.

where is he now?

Africa. he's still in Africa.
I hitched all over Africa. I bummed down there
on a boat. I met a man with a
leopard. he used to take his leopard for a
walk every day on a chain.
one day he didn't show up. his leopard had
eaten him.

that's a funny story.

I think so too. I like you. you understand
things. no more of those young men for me,
those hard bodies. I want you. you're in control
of everything.

I am?

yes, my next husband,
Larry, once covered my body with
rose petals. all those flowers! it was
lovely but he didn't make love to me
again for 2 years. he was such a bad
lover. you're a great
lover.

I am?

yes, wouldn't you like to go to Holland?

no.

to Paris?

no.

to Africa?

no.

Redondo Beach?

no.

you're strange. don't you like to
travel?

I'm sick of that.

you should have seen me fly Retzel's glider!
I was good on that glider.
but he would never go down on
me.

Retzel?

yes, he's a publicist now. he makes good
money.

some day I'll tell you about my
wives.

I don't want to hear about your
wives. I don't want to hear about
any of
them.

she turned over in bed
giving me her back and her
behind.

kid, I said, tell me more about
Retzel.

she turned back toward
me. you really want to
hear?

sure.

then we lay there on our backs
and she talked about Retzel
and I listened.

legs

she arrived in a taxi
completely intoxicated.
it was
after one of my long days as
a May Co. stock boy
and I sat there
exhausted and
sucking at
my beer and
looking at her
in her rumpled state
spread across the bed
skirt hiked high.

I sucked at my drink
then walked over
to the bed and lifted
her skirt higher:
such a sight
those glorious legs
uncovered and helpless.

she was a great woman with
great legs.

we had such tremendous fun
and much agony together
for some years

Rimbaud be damned

it was in Santa Fe.
we sat up waiting for her.
she had gone to some art show or some other
goddamned silly useless thing.

she was a good artist
better than many men
and that was the
problem.

"what the hell happened to Helen?"

"where's Helen?"

Helen's husband, x-husband, was now sitting on the top of a
hill somewhere with a new blue-eyed whore.
quite a
whore: she even wrote
poetry. Vicki was her name. Vicki was now "Mrs."
she had exchanged a rich husband for an even
richer one.

"Helen asked me not to hate Vicki," said my hostess,
"but hell, I can't even like Vicki."

"hell," said my host, "can't you
try?"

"do you like Vicki?" asked my hostess.
Vicki had looked good to me. I couldn't find anything wrong
with her.

"where's Helen?" I asked again. "oh where oh where the hell is
Helen?"

"she'll be here, she'll be here, she said she was
coming."

Helen showed up 3 hours later.
she looked like a snake in a green dress, all fluid,
wild wild, glazed,
her silver necklace pulsating
on her throat
right under my nose.
she was consumed by 3 simple things:
drink, despair, loneliness; and 2 more:
youth and beauty.

it was too much:
I could not withstand the force of
her. I kissed her. I kissed her
again. I was like a schoolboy,
all my toughness
gone.

"let's get the hell out of here!"
I told her, ignoring our host and hostess.

we went next door to her place
and I sat in her kitchen drinking and
watching
her.

"your body, your body, Jesus!" I told
her. she was truly beautiful and laughing,
just like you read about in a novel
only it never really happens to
anybody.

she twisted her body and while humming
did a lovely dance filled with
innuendo.

"baby, I love you," I said, "baby, I love
you!"

we walked down a dark hall hung with a
crucifix and some of her paintings. we entered
another large room. I hung on to my
drink.

"stay here," she said.

I sat on a couch and drank. it seemed
cold and hollow suddenly and
I wondered where she had
gone.

then I looked around and she was lying on another couch
naked and smiling
which was unsettling
for I am used to undressing my
women

and the look of her stark naked there reminded me more of
my slaughterhouse days than
it did of Mozart,
but, of course, who wants to fuck
Mozart?

I finished my drink and undressed and I tried
but I guess I was not much
it was my fault
my fault
and she shoved me
away.

I made a few more halfhearted
tries and then she got up and left.

I also dressed and then
I don't remember much else except
being pretty drunk.

but then when she shoved me out into the rain
I revived.

the rain was wet the rain was cold the rain was
freezing.

"shit," I said, "shit!" I ran back to her
door or to the door I thought was her door
but there seemed to be dozens of doors,
a series of apartments all
enjoined.

I beat on the door I hoped was hers:
"baby, baby, I don't want to fuck you! I realize that I am
a lousy lover! all I want is to get out of this
goddamned rain!"

she didn't reply. I gave up. I ran back to
my first host's apartment. I beat on his door.
it didn't work. the rain was like ice.
I looked into an open garage but it was filled with mud and water;
no place to lie down.

"let me in!" I screamed. "Jesus! mercy! what have I done?
what have I failed to do? YOU ARE YOUR BROTHER'S KEEPER!"

my host came to the door:
"you are a dirty dog!"

"I know, but let me in,
please."

he opened the door and I followed him down the
hall.

"boy oh boy," he said, "you are a son-of-a-bitch, you are
a yellow hound, you aren't worth a damn!"

"I know it," I said.

"did you tell her that I was an x-con?"

"hell, no, I wasn't even thinking of
you."

"then what the hell do you want from
me?"

"nothing. you paid the
train fare down."

"you insulted us both. I don't care about myself but you can't
insult my wife. you said to Helen, 'let's you and I get the
hell out of here, these other people are nothing!' "

"fuck that. you got any whiskey
left?"

"in the refrigerator."

"thanks."

he grunted and climbed into bed beside his
wife.

I brought the bottle out to my cot
and nipped nipped nipped and
listened to the
rain. I thought the night was
over but then he began
again:

"I thought you were a great writer
I thought you were a great man
that's why I paid your fare down here
that's why I published your poetry

that's why I wanted all these people to meet
you!"

"all right," I said, gulping the good whiskey,
"I'll leave in the morning. why don't we all go to
sleep?"

"you are really a son-of-a-bitch!
I never thought you'd be such a son-of-a-bitch!
why do you always keep your eyes half closed?
why can't you look a man in the face?
why do you always avert your glance?"

"I dunno, I dunno."

"you're yellow, that's all: YELLOW!"

I knew it was true
and I took a big hit of whiskey and
said:
"ya wanna go outside and fight?"

"hell! you've got ten years on me!"

"I'll give ya the first
punch!"

"you promise you'll leave in the morning?"

"sure."

    . . .

Helen heard about me leaving
from them I guess
and she came down a little early the next morning to ask if
she could drive me to the little hotel to catch the bus to
the train station.

she still looked good
even more than before
dressed in tight pants and Indian moccasins and
when nobody was looking
I reached over and pinched her
foot. she ignored it but did not tell me to
go to hell
so I felt all warm
inside.

"o.k., I'll drive him down," she said to my
hosts.

"thanks," they said.

I went in to take a
shit.

"we hate to see him go," I heard
my hosts say.

"so do I," she
said.

a big turd dropped
out.

"I'll be back at 2 to pick him up,"
she said.

"goodbye."

"goodbye."

when I came out there were 2 Indians sitting there
with my hosts.
the Chief said, "I trusted that nigger with 8 bucks
for 2 four-pound sacks of chili beans. it's been 2
weeks and he ain't back yet. he worked for some cement company.
lemme have your phone book, I'm gonna find that
bastard!"

they introduced me to his squaw. I kissed her on the
cheek. she giggled. she was about 60 years old and had
bad legs.

"I got problems," said the Chief, and
then he ripped the blanket off my cot
and wrapped it around and around himself.
"I am big Chief," he said, "all I need is a
good piece of ass and then to catch that nigger."

"don't look at me," I told him, "I am
neither."

the Chief looked at
me. "I think I need a bath,"
he said.

he went and climbed into one of the 3 tubs in one of the
3 bathrooms. then the squaw decided that she also needed a
bath. and then somebody else decided they had to take a
shit. they all vanished. I drank my drink and went back to
sleep.

   . . .

"we are so sorry to see you go," a
voice said, waking me.

the Indians had left.

"it's all right," I
said.

I didn't get any
argument.

I got into the car with Helen and the sight
of her nylon knees beat hammers into my brain.
I was so sorry that I would never possess anything good,
anything like her,
that nothing good would ever belong to me
not because I was always poor in dollars
but because I was poor at expressing myself one-on-one.
I was as yellow as the sun perhaps
but also as warm and as true as the sun
somewhere there inside me
but nobody would ever find it.

I would certainly end up forever crying the blues into a
coffee cup in a park for old men playing

chess or silly games of some sort.
shit! shit!
and then Helen shifted the gears and we rolled down through the
rich hills and there was nothing I could say to her
about her beauty or how tough I was
or that just to sit and look at her for a month
never to touch her again
would be my only desire
but like a bastard I was probably lying to myself
I probably wanted everything everything
but now at 45
having lived with a dozen women and loving none
I was now crazy, finished. as she
drove me through the hills everything screamed inside of
me, and I kept saying as we drove along
(to myself, of course)
fucker, it will pass,
everything passes,
it's all a joke
a joke on you,
forget it, think of dead dogs dead things think of
yourself: unwanted, broke, simple, a supposed poet writing of
deep things, but you can't really write about anything except
YOURSELF. isn't it true? isn't it true? you are a prick,
a self-centered jackass only wanting an easy way out? you crave
money, grandstands full of applause, recognition and a book
of poems that will still be admired in the year 2,179.

you are a
shit-yellow screaming jackal: you ain't gonna make it and
you might as well get used to it
now.

we drove up to the little hotel
and the poor jackass poet said,
"may I say goodbye?" it was
like a bad movie, only it wasn't a movie:
I could understand Dos's *Crime and Punishment*
I could understand the moon leaning across a bar on skid row
and asking for a drink, but I couldn't understand anything about
    myself,
I was murdered, I was shit, I was a tentful of dogs,
I was poppies mowed down by machine-gun fire
I was a hotshot wasp in a web
I was less and less and still reaching for
something, and I thought of her corny remark
a night or so ago:
"you have wounded eyes."
corny, of course, but anything that comes from a real
woman is not corny
and I thought of her decent paintings of people and things
reaching wanting wanting
and like a shell-shocked Jap surrounded by heroic
American troops
I kissed her
goodbye.

"I'm sorry I couldn't make it good for you,"
she said. "I wasn't ready, I guess."
"no, it was my fault,"
I told her.

I walked into the little hotel in that
small town (from where they took you to the train
via bus) and I got lost, shit, I got lost,

I couldn't find the ticket office, up and
down steps
in and out of doors
tears again finally
like a bad movie again, and
finally I found the ticket agent
and went through the business
of buying a ticket.

I went and sat in the lobby and
I looked up from my ticket
and there she was.
"what are you doing here?" I asked.

"I saw you all hunched up and sad and cold.
I kept thinking of you."

the bus to the train was late, everything was
late, so she drove me around town meanwhile and I had to go through the
whole thing again with her.

and I knew that even the proper words would never do
the trick. I was dirty, dirt, I looked like dirt,
I was dirty, dirty dirt. I just wanted to get inside of her,
stay there, I was nothing but a cunt-wanter and
I was broke. I couldn't spell, I didn't even know about using
2 or 3 forks at dinner, I didn't know anything about Harvard or
diplomas or 50 grand a year, and she knew that all that
was true: I had been kicked around for too long, I no longer
knew the way up or out or even wanted to know: I was destined for
failure.

I said goodbye again
sucking up all that was left of her into the
little that was left of
me. I said, "don't look for me again. fuck it.
we are all lost. goodbye, goodbye."

she was great. she drove off. I watched that last flash
of her go around the corner and disappear and
then I walked back into the hotel lobby.

they were chummy, 5 or 6 assholes still sitting and
waiting there.

2 were doctors. another was the possessor of something great
and important. they all had wives. it was beginning to
snow.

we all climbed into the bus to go to the
train. I was already numb,
numb again,
numb
again
again and again,
numbness and pain swelling in
me—just like in the good
old times.

the Mexican drove down the road and almost stripped the
gears.

the comfortable people made comfortable jokes
about weather and things
but I sat mostly silent
saying a word or so when necessary
a word or so
trying to hide from them the fact that I was a fool
and feeling terrible
and the small hills began to be covered with snow
slowly things became white
slowly things became whiter
and I knew that it all would finally pass
and thank the good grace of the good God,
my years and time were running
out; we drove on and on,
past little villages and both good things and
bad things were happening to the
people in those villages too,
but I still was nothing
but arms and ears and eyes and maybe there'd be
either some good luck for me or
more death tomorrow.

bewitched in New York

the lady was the most unfaithful and terrible I had
ever encountered and I knew it and she knew it and she was
both ugly and beautiful at the same time and the
two of her just sat there on the window
ledge of that open hotel window
in New York City on
one of the hottest days of all time, no
air-conditioning, no fan, we sweated and
suffered and waited for something
to happen.

I was drunk, she was on drugs, we had just
concluded a slippery bit of
copulation and afterward she said, "you son-of-a-
bitch, we're stuck here in hell!"

"good," I said.

then I saw her fall out of the window, we
were four floors up, I heard the scream,
her body was gone.

then it was back, she was sitting on the
window ledge again. "did you see that?" she
asked. "I fell out of the window!"

"good," I said.

"but somehow I pulled myself back in!" she
said.

"good," I said.

"is that all you can say?" she asked.
" 'good'?"

"I can say that I think you're a witch or a devil
and that your window act just now proves
it."

I felt that by falling out she had lifted my
spirits and then she had deliberately dashed
them by climbing back
in.

"so I'm a witch or a devil, huh? well, no more
ass for you!"

"good," I said.

sometimes you live and stay with a woman and have no
real idea why.

with her I knew: it was the simple, fascinating,
unrelenting mystery and terror of
her self.

don't worry, baby, I'll get it

he saw her in a liquor store
and it shook him
shook shook shook
like shark meat alive still in sunlight flopping.

he hurled his eyes at her,
a miracle, he heard her talking to him,
she was funny, she made him laugh, she made him feel like
all the doors were open for him.

it was easy. she went back to his place with him.
they talked. it was easy. she was a glorious fuck. they
fucked 3 times. she
stayed.

"Smaltz," they phoned him from work the next day,
"what ya doin', ya didn't come
in! we got the Granger-Wently order to get
out: 45 six-foot squeegees and 90 gallons of
ultramarine Day-Glo!"

"I'm busy," he said, and they replied,
"we can get a shipping clerk
anywhere!" he hung up, turned her over and
fucked her
again.

it wasn't the same as with the others:
every time he finished he felt he wanted more.
as she took the trip to the bathroom it seemed as if he
hadn't yet really had her, and anything she put on,

a newspaper hat, a pair of his socks, she looked
glorious, funny funny, hell, she made him feel good,
everything she said, shit, was a
joke. she'd put that body up against his every morning and
say, "ah, don't go ta work, Eddie baby, stay wit me!"
"I can't go to work, sweets, I don't have no job," he'd say,
and they'd go at it
again.

so the day came: no rent, no coffee, no wine, no
cigarettes. the landlord stated: one more day;
get it up or get it out—!

"shit, I thought you knew what you were doing,"
she told Smaltz. it was the first time she wasn't
funny.

"don't worry, baby, I'll get it," he told
her, and they went one last good one.

lucky, he had the .32. he thought, liquor store, no, I'll get the
big stuff, she's got it
comin', she's for me, mine, paper hat, all that
shaking, god, nothing like
it.

he tried the bank. the big gray one nearby.
he went in. he was ready: .32, paper bag, the note:
"a stickup. quiet and you don't die. no buttons. put money in
bag. I am desperate and will kill. please let us both live."

she emptied the drawer into the bag. he saw it:
lots of hundreds, fifties. sweet mother. a trip to Paris.
the bank clerk looked good too. he'd like to fuck
her. anybody would.

he was almost at the door
when he sensed she'd tripped the button right
away. they'd even cleared the
crowd. the guard at the door was easy—
he was so fat Smaltz couldn't miss:
he dropped like a putty freak.

outside he saw the squad car;
the thing was driving along the wrong side of
the street—how could they do that?—
keeping even as he was running,
and firing at his ass,
coming close; he ran up an alley, dead end,
but he caught a freight elevator
at the bottom, "move it up! MOVE IT UP!"
he shouted at another freak
but the freak just stood there
looking at the .32, and he shot the freak,
nothing else to do,
and he was working at the handles, trying to
close the doors
when they got there, fired at him,
fired into that cheap tin elevator; he couldn't get off a
return shot. they got him, took the paper bag out of his
hand.

the next night she was sleeping with the owner of a
hardware store, Harry, a good solid income, 2 fingers
missing from his right hand—hunting accident in Indiana,
1938.

you could get another shipping clerk
anywhere.

the telephone message machine

is one of the world's greatest
inventions.

seldom do I pick up the phone
to interrupt the
message
and speak directly to the
caller.

and I hardly ever phone
anybody
these days
nor did I in the
past
unless it was some new girlfriend
who had me by the
balls.

and she never had an
answering machine
just pills
unpaid bills
neglected children
many pressing needs
and an utterly overvalued sense of her
self,
especially by
me.

that nice girl who came in to change the sheets

I met her when she came in to
change the sheets.
St. Louis.
she told me: you're sick.
and I said:
yes, I'm sick.
and she said:
you need something to drink
I came to change the sheets
but you need something to drink
give me some money and
I'll come back with something to
drink.
so
I gave her the money
not knowing her
but she came back with something to
drink.
she sat in a chair and I
stayed in bed and we drank
silently.
and then we began to talk
and then we laughed a little
and I began to feel better and she
looked better
and I said:
I didn't think you'd come back
and she said:
hell, I work here.
and I said:
o, that's why you came
back.

and she said:
no, that's not why I came back.
and
I liked that.

I hardly remember how it happened
but we were soon both in bed
smoking cigarettes and drinking
beer
out of those heavy quart
jugs.
there seemed no hurry.

and then it began to
work. I don't know how it worked
but it was all right. we
fucked.
and she got up and closed the windows to the south
and said:
that's what's killing you
those gas fumes coming up from the avenue
that
and the drinking. at least we can get you
away from the gas fumes.
we laughed and then she got back in bed and we
talked some more and smoked and she
got out of bed and said
she had to go—
her boyfriend lived downstairs with her,
and I said goodbye

and she left and
then I looked over at the chair
and I saw the clean white sheets.
she had forgotten to change the sheets
so I got up and
changed the sheets for her.

an agreement on Tchaikovsky

both my legs are broken at the knees
and I can't move my right arm:
it's Spring and the birds are popping
in and out of the brush
driving the cats crazy.

my good friend, Randy, frequents the
men's crappers at the racetrack
looking for wallets: smart boy:
if his folks had been rich
he tells me he would have gone
on to Harvard.

she keeps playing Tchaikovsky's 4th,
the one that goes
ka plunk plunk plunk plunk plunk;
I don't like it
but old lady Rose
my neighbor
at the Sunset Park Rest Home
thinks it's
beautiful.

everybody's too old here to use
the tennis court
there's a layer of dust over the whole thing
and the net's a bunch of busted string.

old lady Rose went to visit her kids today—
that is, they came and *got* her, the old bag;
she can't walk at all
and her legs aren't even busted—

she's just a tiresome old
fart!

I wheeled myself into her room a while back
and found a 10-dollar bill folded real neat
and tight;
she thought nobody'd find it
in one of her old slippers
but I've been around
and she'll come knocking on *my* door tonight
asking for a "little touch of scotch";
man, all that crap about the land she USED
to own in Arizona and how her husband USED
to wear spats and carry a cane!
he don't need to wear anything where he's at now;
and while I was in there
I cracked old Tchaikovsky #4 across the arm of a chair
broke it good.
and old lady Rose was right:
it sounded damned beautiful to me:
something like
the cracking of walnuts.

love song to the woman I saw Wednesday
at the racetrack

remembering Savannah 20 years ago
a four poster bed
and streets full of helmets and hunters
things I did then
left welts;
ha ha, you say,
but they come alive as I buy bread
or lace a shoe
and it doesn't matter
except that it works for me
like the legs of that woman worked for me
as the sun works for me as it works for the cactus
and as you work for me
reading this poem.

and the legs of that woman walk
as I watch them
and the horses in the next race
and the mountains stand there
watching

welts and a woman's legs
10-win on number six
and out in the ocean
or standing in the park
like a statue
I watch her
walking.

horses standing everywhere:
Savannah-like seashells in my pocket:
I have loved you woman
as surely as I have named you
rust and sand and nylon.

you have worked for me

wild thing.

possession

an old woman talks to a girl who is
drying her long black hair while sitting on a back step,
she points her finger and speaks in a foreign tongue
and the sun is very beautiful
as the old woman talks and combs the tangled strands
(so many moons have gone down before and since).
suddenly the young girl cries out and shakes her head
and together they go back into the house
where together they will die,
but don't they understand
it was mine, not theirs:
the hair, the long black sun-dried hair,
and maybe the girl too?

six

10:30 a.m.
5 coffee drinkers at the Pickwick Café
the boys who work the horse stables
at Hollywood Park
turn in their swivel seats
together,
one, two, three, four, five,
they turn
leaving their cooling coffees and their
small talk
to stare at a girl walking by
who comes in and sits in a booth.
it is hardly an unusual girl,
just a girl,
and one, two, three, four,
four of them turn back to their coffees;
the 5th, a young healthy blond boy
continues to look
with his nice vacant blue eyes.
then, at last, he turns back to his coffee.
it has to be more than it appears, I think,
ah yes, let me see,
they are thinking, that's the one who fucked Mick
out behind the stables last night.
yes, yes, of course, they are punishing her
for not fucking *them*.
nasty boys; little horse turd egos.
they all believe they have cocks like stallions.
"another coffee?" the waitress asks me.
"yes, thanks," I say, thinking, I should get a
better look at that girl
myself.

man mowing the lawn across the way from me

I watch you walking with your machine.
ah, you're too stupid to be cut like grass,
you're too stupid to let anything violate you—
the girls won't use their knives on you
they don't want to
their sharp edge is wasted on you,
you are interested only in baseball games and
western movies and grass blades.

can't you take just one of my knives?
here's an old one—stuck into me in 1955,
she's dead now, it wouldn't hurt much.
I can't give you this last one—
I can't pull it out yet,
but here's one from 1964, how about taking
this 1964 one from me?

man mowing the lawn across the way from me
don't you have a knife somewhere in your gut
where love left?

man mowing the lawn across the way from me
don't you have a knife somewhere deep in your heart
where love left?

man mowing the lawn across the way from me
don't you see the young girls walking down the sidewalks now
with knives in their purses?
don't you see their beautiful eyes and dresses and
hair?
don't you see their beautiful asses and knees and
ankles?

man mowing the lawn across the way from me
is that all you see—those grass blades?
is that all you hear—the drone of the mower?

I can see all the way to Italy
                    to Japan
                    to Honduras
I can see the young girls sharpening their knives
in the morning and at noon and at night, and
especially at night, o,
especially at night.

the girl outside

it is 1:30 p.m.
Monday
65 degrees in November
on Western Avenue.
a girl walks out of a doorway
and stands in front.
an older woman comes out and leans
against the doorway.
the girl is in her early twenties
dressed in a short buttoned-up
red dress. she has on panty hose and
orange slippers
and gives the appearance of one
who has just awakened.
she grins in the afternoon.
she does a short sexy dance and grins.
she is pale. she is blonde.
suddenly she waves at somebody passing
in a car.
life is interesting.
she is young.
she is a girl.
she dances again. she waves. she
grins.
that's all very nice for 1:30 in the
afternoon at 65 degrees.
she wants money.
she waves. she dances.
she grins.
the older woman is bored and walks back
inside.

I start my car in the parking lot across the
street.
I drive west down Oakwood and no longer see
the girl.
it's so strange. I think,
we all need money.
then I turn on the radio and try to
forget about
that.

the chicken

I came by, she said,
and I hung this roasted chicken on your doorknob
and two days later it was still hanging there
swinging in the wind.
you should have seen that thing!
and your car was outside
and the chicken kept swinging
and I said to my husband,
what's that stink?
he must be dead.
the wind was really blowing that
chicken around, you should have seen that
chicken swing, and I told my husband,
that crazy son-of-a-bitch must be dead
in there.
so he got the key and we went in.

yeah, I said, what did you find?

just empty bottles and garbage. you
were gone. you weren't in
there.

did you look in all the closets?

we looked everywhere, under the bed,
everywhere.

I wonder where I was?

I dunno. where did you get that big scab on your head?

I was toasting a marshmallow on a coat hanger
and burned my fore-
head.

oh, I thought maybe somebody hit you.

uh-uh, I said, uh-uh.

an ancient love

I don't remember our ages:
we must have been between 5 and 7,
there was this girl next door about my age.
I do remember her name: Lila Jane.
and one thing she would do every day,
once a day, was to ask me:
"are you ready?"
and I would indicate that I was
and she would lift her dress and
show me her panties and they were
a different color each day.

several decades later she somehow found me
and came by with her boyfriend
some fellow who smoked a pipe
and who read my books
and she crossed her long beautiful legs
high
but not high enough for me to see the panties.

and when they were ready to leave
I gave her a hug and
I shook hands with her boyfriend
and I never saw him or her
or her panties
ever again.

match point

read in the paper where a 72-year-old wife strangled her
91-year-old husband with his
necktie.
she said the age difference was
unbearable and added that
when they had met on a tennis court 30 years
earlier
the age gap had not seemed
important.

it looks like I've been in serious danger
at least a half dozen times
in the last 25 years or so and still
am.

there's just one necktie in my
closet, purchased it to go to a funeral
not long ago,
but I've never played
tennis and don't intend to
try.

I also like to look at ceilings

there are policemen in the street
and angels in the clouds
and jockeys riding in their silks.

down through the mornings
up through the nights
parallel to the afternoons
there are crippled dogs in
East Kansas City
vampires in Eugene, Oregon
and a long walk for a glass of water in the
Twin Cities.

I meant to write Angela
I really did
and thank her for everything
because I sincerely
liked the way she draped shawls on her
staircase
and her herb tea
and the green vines in her
bathroom
the view from her bedroom
and her collection of
Vivaldi.

but I didn't.

I guess I'm crueler than
I think I am.

no Cagney, me

I had a borrowed tv set for a month
and saw some old Cagney movies.

much of Cagney's interaction with women
takes place in the kitchen.
they say something he doesn't
like. he slaps them with a dish towel
or pushes a grapefruit into their
face. they weep and fall
into his arms.

me, I am always being attacked by
women
especially when I am discouraged or
tired. they push me out of doorways
into the rain, into mud puddles on my
back. they pour beer over my head
come at me with knives and bookends
they attack
snarling like the leopard
they rip my coats and shirts
apart.
they attack me at the moment
I am casually talking to a
friend or while I am
asleep. sometimes they also beat their heads
against the wall.

I'm leaving, I say.

oh, you always want to end it,
don't you?

well, Christ, you act like you don't
like it.

well, go then, go!

I go. no Cagney, me. I drive away
thinking, oh shit, God, it's so nice to
be alone again.

you had it, Jimmy.
what a woman wants is a
reaction.
what a man wants is a
woman.

you're best.

soup, cosmos and tears

I've known some crazy women
but the craziest was
Annette
and it seems the crazier they are
the better the lay,
and what bodies they
have. Annette always lived with
Chinese men
but you never saw them
that's what scared you,
even the Mafia is scared of the Chinese—
"where's the dragon, kid?"
"that's all right. he knows you're all right."
"you sure? when they put the X on you,
you might as well
forget it."
"I told them you were all right. that's all
they need."
Annette had incense burning,
all sorts of charts and weirdo books,
she always talked about the gods
she had a direct line to the gods.
"you have been selected by the gods," she told
me.
"o.k., babe, let's make it
then."
"not right now. I want you to try this special soup
I've made."
"special soup?"
"yes, eat it and you will inherit the forces of
earth and sun, the entire
cosmos."

I went and ate the soup. frankly, it tasted all right,
though a bit rusty. no telling what the hell she had
put in there. I finished
it.
"I feel like a man of steel
now."
"you have inherited the force," she said, "the gods are
proud of you."
on the couch I finally got hold of
her. under that loose orange gown
was enough woman to kill an
ox.
"I lived in that hotel in Paris," she said. "I slept with all of
them. Burroughs, the whole
gang. I knew Pound at St. Liz."
"you slept with Ezra?"
"more than any!"
"oh fuck!"
"go," she laughed, "ahead."

it had been good
soup. those Paris boys and
Ezra had known a good
mare.
I rolled
off.

when she came out of the bathroom she
had a bottle in her hand and began sprinkling me
with the
contents.
"hey, what's this shit?"

"the tears of the
gods."
"the tears of the gods?"
"yes, the tears of the
gods."
I laid there until she was
finished.
then I got up and
dressed.

"when can I see you
again?"

"in 2 hours or
tomorrow."

I walked to the door.

"you walk like a
poem," she said.
"see you in 2
hours," I told
her.

the door closed. what a man had to go through for a
piece of ass
in this modern age was
highly
suspect.

peacock or bell

I am laughing mouth closed;
as I turn the pages of my newspaper
it's like a symphony gone wrong;
seeing much to make me doubt
flashing there across the page
it's like a cheap movie gone haywire;
my clothing sits in chairs
like the dead emptied out,
husks of things wrinkling the vision;
it's colder than hell (yes) but
the blankets are thin,
and the pulled-down shades
are as full of holes as love is.
I think you've got to be a sportsman;
yes, for the sportsman it's all right:
you just crack out the gun
and blow the head off something
perhaps off the maiden sitting in
the chair that grandma sat in,
but not having a gun,
I go to the phone
and phone a woman as old as the chair and grandma,
and she promises to come and charm me;
she has a toothbrush but no teeth
and I will probably dance naked for her
my blob of belly a white sack.
each man has his own way out: mine is doubtful
but has been working well of late
and the music of it sometimes frightens me,

but then
I wake up, buy a paper,
kick a can,
pull up the shade,
start again.

purple and black

a girl in purple pants and black sweater
crossing the street
with a camper and high-rise background,
a Saturday afternoon graveyard Hollywood
background,
is quite interesting:
something moving,
something moving in purple and black as
her hair waves in the wind as she turns,
the sun like the eye of a frog,
winter is where it's at
here, and the street is insipid, vapid,
I could pound myself against that asphalt until
I bled mad
and it wouldn't care;
the girl in purple and black
gives the street destination and direction
until she is out of range of my window,
and now it is again
what it was, and a small spider
almost like something made out of a lost hair,
an eyelid hair,
crawls along the wall to my left
and I don't have even the desire to
kill it. outside my window
it is ghost-shivered and
stinks of the malice of men.
I wait for new arrangements

but meanwhile endure
as the phone rings
as I leap from my chair
like a man shot in the
back.

fulfillment

she disciplined herself in
anger
hatred and cunning
strategy.

I always thought that it would
finally pass
that she was giddy with
misconception and bad
advice.

I always felt it would
pass.

I listened to the charges against me
knowing some of them to be true
but certainly not
important enough
to become the target of
violence, envy,
vengeance.

I thought it would surely
pass.

I commandeered no
defense
thinking that easy
reason
would save us
both

but her determination
strengthened—
even then
I summed it up as headstrong, over-
zealous
energy

but the moment I gave ground
more ground was
taken.

lord, I thought, it's just simple
violence

and so I trotted my horse
out of the stable
sharpened my knives and
began a
counterattack.

she'd finally found
as good an opponent as could be
found.

her determination demanded her own
destruction.

she'd found her
match
I mounted my steed
sword ready
ready even for the sun.

she'd always wanted war
I'd grant her wish
love be damned now
as love was damned when it
first arrived.

my reluctance would
now be gone
forever

and the blood
would flow

hers and mine

just as she desired.

yours

my women of the past keep trying to locate me.
I duck into dark closets and pull the overcoats
over my head.

at the racetrack I sit in the clubhouse
smoking cigarette after cigarette
watching the horses come out for the post parade
and looking over my shoulder.

I go to bet and this one's ass looks like that one's
ass used to.
I duck away from her.

then that one's hair might have her under it.
I get the hell out of the clubhouse and go
to the grandstand.

I don't want a return of the past.
I don't want a return of those
ladies of my past,
I don't want to try again, I don't want to see
them again even in silhouette;
I give them all, all of them to all the other eager
men, they can have those darlings,
those tits those asses those thighs those minds
and their mothers and fathers and sisters and
brothers and children and dogs and x-boyfriends
and current boyfriends, they can have them all and
fuck them all
if they want to.

I was a terrible and jealous lover who mistreated
and failed to understand
them and it's best that they are with others now
for that will be better for them and that will be
better for me
so when they phone or write or leave
messages
I will forward them all to their new
fine fellows.

I don't deserve what they have and I want to
keep it that way.

kissing me away

she was always thinking about it
and she was young and beautiful and
all my friends were jealous:
what was an old fuck like me
doing with a young girl like
her?

she was always thinking about
it.

we'd be driving along and
she'd say, "see that little
place? park over there."

I'd hardly get parked and
she'd be down on me.

once I drove her to Arizona
and halfway there
late at night
after coffee and doughnuts
at an all-night joint
she bent over
and started in
while I was navigating the
dark curves through the
low hills
and as I kept driving
it inspired her to
new heights.

another time
in L.A.
we'd purchased hot dogs and cokes
and fries and we were eating in
Griffith Park
families there
children playing
and she unzipped me
and started in.

"what the hell are you doing?"
I asked her.

later
when I asked her
why
in front of everybody
she told me it was
dangerous and thrilling
that way.

she asked me one
time, "why am I staying with an
old guy like you
anyhow?"

"so you can give me blow
jobs?" I replied.

"I *hate* that term!" she
said.

"sucking me off," I
suggested.

"I hate that term
too!" she said.

"what would you prefer?"
I asked.

"I like to think that
I'm 'kissing you away,' "
she said.

"all right," I said.

   . . .

it was like any other
relationship, there was
jealousy on both sides,
there were split-ups and
reconciliations.
there were also fragmented moments of
great peace and beauty.

I often tried to get away from her and
she tried to get away from me
but it was difficult:
Cupid, in his strange way, was really
there.

whenever I had to leave town
she kissed me away

good
a couple of nights in a
row
ensuring my
fidelity.

then all I had to
do was
worry about
her.

when she wasn't
kissing me away
we also found time
to do it
in several other strange
ways.

but all that time with
her it
was mostly just
being
kissed away or
waiting to be.

we never thought about
much else.
we never went to
movies (which I hated
anyhow).
we never ate
out.

we were not curious
about
world affairs.
we just spent our time
parked in
secluded places or picnic
grounds or
driving dark
roads to New Mexico,
Nevada and Utah.

or
we were in her big oak
bed
facing south
so much of the rest of the
time
that I memorized
each wrinkle in the
drapes
and especially
all the cracks in the
ceiling.

I used to play games with
her with that ceiling.

"see those cracks up
there?"

"where?"

"look where I'm pointing . . ."

"o.k."

"now, see those cracks, see the
pattern? it forms an image. do you see
what it is?"

"umm, umm . . ."

"go on, what is it?"

"I know! it's a man on top of a
woman!"

"wrong. it's a flamingo standing
by a stream."

   . . .

we finally got free of
one another.
it's sad but it's
standard operating procedure
(I am constantly confused by
the lack of durability in human
affairs).

I suppose the parting was
unhappy
maybe even ugly.
it's been 3 or 4
years now

and I wonder if she
ever thinks of
me, of what I am
doing?

of course, I know what she's
doing.

and she did it better
than anybody
I ever knew.

and I guess that's worth this
poem, maybe.

if not, then at least a
footnote: that such affairs are
not without joy and humor for both
parties
and as Saigon and the enemy tanks get
scrambled in old dreams
as old and infirm dogs get
killed crossing roads
as the drawbridge rises to let
the drunken fishermen out to
sea
it wasn't for nothing
that
she was thinking
about it
all the
time.

goodbye, my love

deadly ash of everything
we've mauled it to pieces
ripped the head off
the arms
the legs
cut away the sexual organs
pissed on the heart

deadly ash of everything
everywhere
the sidewalks are now harder
the eyes of the populace crueler
the music more tasteless

ash
I'm left with pure
ash

first we pissed on the heart
now we piss on the ash.

heat

if you have ever drawn up your last plan on
an old shirt cardboard in an Eastside hotel room of winter
with last week's rent due and a dead radiator
you'll know how large small things are
like yourself coming up the stairway
maybe for the final time
with your bottle of wine
thinking of the lady in #9
putting on her garters
and on her dresser there is a
dark red drinking glass
which catches the overhead light like a
soft dream of Jerusalem
and she dusts herself
slips into silk and sheath and
spiked feet
and unemployed and looking for work
and maybe looking for you
she passes you on the
stairway;
such disturbing grace
transforms one.
like a blue-winged fly exploding into
the summer sky
you decide to hang around and
die later; you enter your room and pour wine like
blood, inward, and decide in the morning you'll
get up early and
read the want
ads.

the police helicopter

the police helicopter keeps circling over the yard
"what do they want?" I ask her.
"they're probably looking for you," she says.
this is not as far-fetched as you might think:
I went into a bar one night with some friends
and the owner came out from around the bar
and asked to speak to me.
"I don't know if we can serve you or not,
you must promise to be good,
you created quite a fuss the last time you
were here."
I promised him to be good and that night
I drank under a great deal of strain.

anyhow, the helicopter keeps circling
and it is one o'clock in the afternoon
but the night before it had circled and circled
shining its beam into the backyard
and into the crapper.
it had circled for 45 minutes, then
had left.

now it is back.
"what the hell?" I say,
"they want you," she says,
"this is ridiculous," I say.
I walk into the backyard.
there's nothing out there:
walnut trees, bamboo stalks, a discarded
sofa and grass 3 feet high.
I stand out there and watch the helicopter

circling, circling.
it finally leaves.

I come back in.
"I feel like John Dillinger," I say.
"you look like John Dillinger," she says.
I walk to the mirror.
it's true:
I look like John Dillinger,
but no woman in a red dress could ever
finger me. I'm
too smart.

ah

flamingo pain,
burnt fingers trying to
light the last of this
joint
in a place described
by terrified ladies
with money in their purses
as a "rat hole."

"you can spit on the floor here,"
I tell them.

but no, from
a safe
distance, it appears
they'd rather discuss
my poetry.

of course

according to the latest scientific
study
it takes 325 years for the last
brain cell
to pop.

now I realize that
most of the girls
I met in bars
and brought home with me
were lying about
their
age.

the dream, the dream

there is always some new Carmen just around
some corner
somewhere
but then the Carmens never seem to
last;
the Carmens hardly last any time at
all.
I see this in the eyes of men
everywhere—
men sitting at lunch counters
men driving buses
men giving political speeches
men pulling teeth
men in tiger cages
men I see everywhere . . .

the man I see while I shave
looks back at me through slit-eyes
his Carmen also gone—
that man (me) is now
thinking about what that
razor might really
do, the thought is always
there—

but the game keeps us
going: there is always some new Carmen
waiting
somewhere
just around some
corner.

note on the tigress

first, a terrible argument.
next, we made love.
now, at last, I lay peacefully
on her large bed
which is
spread with a field of gracious flowers,
my head and belly down,
head sideways,
sprayed by shaded light
as she bathes quietly in the
other room.
it is all beyond me
as are most things.
I listen to classical music on a small radio.
she bathes.
I hear the splashing of water.

three

while most people

converse it all away

I

write it down.

poem for my daughter

I spoon it
in: strained chicken noodle dinner
junior prunes
junior fruit dessert.

spoon it in and
for Christ's sake
don't blame the
child
don't blame the
govt.
don't blame the bosses or the
working classes—

spoon it down
into that little mouth
like melted
wax.

a friend phones:
"whatya gonna do now, Hank?"
"what the hell ya mean, what am I gonna
do?"
"I mean ya got responsibility now, ya gotta bring the
kid up
right."

I feed her instead:
spoon it in!
may she achieve
a place in Beverly Hills
with never any need for unemployment compensation

and never have to sell to the highest
bidder.

and never fall in love with a soldier or a killer of any
kind.

and may she
appreciate Beethoven and Jelly Roll Morton and
beautiful dresses.

she's got a real
chance:
there was once the
Theoric Fund and now there's the
Great Society.

"are ya still gonna play the horses? are ya still gonna
drink? are ya still gonna—?"

"yes."

she is a waving flower in the wind and the dead center of
my heart—
now she sleeps beautifully like a
boat on the Nile.

maybe some day she will
bury me.

that would be nice

if it weren't a
responsibility.

sheets

those sheets you've got there,
said the old dame
in the housewares dept.,
are for a double bed.
do you have a double bed or a
single bed?
well, you see, I answered,
my bed is an unusual bed, it's
kind of a single-and-a-
half.
describe your bed, she said.
what?
describe your
bed.
I'd rather not, I said.
well, said the old dame, I want you to
know the sheets you've got there are
for a double bed, and if you've got a single
bed, it's against the state
law.
what? I asked. say that
again.
I said, it's against the state
law.
you mean? I asked.
I mean, you can't bring these sheets back
after you've opened the
package.
all right, I said, give me a couple of
singles.
she treated me then with comfortable
disdain. I believe the old dame had been in

sheets all her
life. I think they should put young girls
in the sheets dept.
after all, sheets don't make me think of sleep
at all
but something else
entirely. especially crisp white new
sheets.
they ought to put old dames like her in
dog food. or garden supplies. and
when she gave me the singles I knew she knew I slept
alone. like she
did.

sick leave

there I am flat on my belly, Hem is dead, Shake is dead,
the fish I have caught and eaten and shitted are dead
and the doc is ramming a glass tube up my ass,
a glass tube with a little light on the end of it,
and I am hoping for a medical excuse
for 2 more days of sick leave
and the doc plays right along: "ya got some beauts there,
you oughta be cut . . ." well, the White Russians used to
cut a hole in a man and take hold of the end of the intestine
and nail it to a tree and then force the man to
run around and around the tree.

he pulls the glass tube out of my ass
and part of me along with it
he has a face like a walnut and when his nurse
bends over (which is often)
her butt is like a big soft pillow or
powdered doughnut, no blood, just clouds,
and I say, "Doc, add a day to the excuse,
I can feel the pain all the way down to my nuts . . ."
"sure," he says, "sure, I know a lot of boys
from the Post Office, all nice boys."

at home I screw the cap off the bottle
and have the first good one; it rained while he rammed me:
the rain sits glittering in the screen
like sugar flies eating dreams,
and I split the Racing Form with my thumb,
then call my bookie,
". . . give me 2 across on Indian Blood,
5 win on Lady Fanfare, 5 place on The Rage."

I hang up and think softly of Kafka
sleeping under the paws of gophers
as the lady across the hall sings to her canary.

love has clicked off and on
like a cigarette lighter
and now her love is a
bird.

it gets like that when not much happens
and you play on a small stage,
and I pin my medical exemption to
the front of one of my old paintings
rub some salve up my ass
and pour another drink.

my father

my father liked rules and doing things
the hard way.
he spoke of responsibilities and laws
and things that just *had* to be done correctly.
a man must work, a man must eat.
a man must own property and mow his lawn.

I turned out to be a drunkard and wanderer
and his hard-packed letters followed me everywhere.
I watched the pigeons in the rain in
New Orleans while his letters said,
get going, *make* something of yourself!

how hard the world tries and how hard
everything has been for me.
my father is old and gray now and when
I walk into his house he complains
about the mud I track in. he
is proud of his house and garden and
he sits back and waits. but I
am horrified as he speaks to me:
he has never thought of death! he does
not think of dying! as he talks, his
mouth is a round hole; he leans back content
upon his pillows. when I leave he says,
come again, come again.

how many times and why?
who is my father? did he ever
play a mandolin or swim the icy waters?
I know my father: he is dead. there is dead
mud and there is a tree branch. the tree

branch works easily in the wind and
between the leaves you see glimpses of the sun.
it's quiet. it's real. it's warm.
and the mud on the floor is my father's heart
and his brain.

the old woman

she lived in the last old house
on the block—
you know the kind: vine-covered, dark, quiet.
her neighbors were gone—
nothing but high-rise apartments everywhere.
you'd see her two or three times a week
pushing her little shopping cart on its two wheels;
then she'd come back with stuff in bags,
go into the house, and that was
it. she never spoke to anybody.

it was last week about 3:30 p.m.
that her house began sliding off its foundation.
it was a very slow slide
and you got the idea that the house was just stepping
forward to take a walk down the street—
except some of the lumber began to snap—
it sounded like rifle shots, and the house moaned just a
little—a dark green moan.

somebody called the fire dept.
and men were running around shutting off the gas
and shouting at each other
and telling the crowd to keep back
and along came one of those television trucks
and they filmed the house
sagging toward the street.

then the front door opened and the little old
lady came out.
they put the camera on her and a woman ran up with a
mike.

"how long have you been living in your house?"

"55 years."

"do you have insurance?"

"no."

"what will you do
now?"

"go back to Ireland," she said.

then she walked away and left them all just standing
there.

what made you lose your inspiration?

Norman is drizzling off into a self-pleased
imbecility as he sits on my couch and
giggles, pulls at his
diseased beard
and talks about his girlfriend Katrinka,
Eugene Debs, F. Scott Fitzgerald and
LSD.
a bad writer, almost unpublished, this
gives him strength as
he sits there and tells me
that my own writing has gone way down
from volcanic burst to cigarette-lighter
flash.
I give him something to drink and
he gets down on the floor and
begins talking into my tape machine.
I light a cigar and
listen.
"I want to be the Number One Writer of Our
Time. I want to walk down the street and hear people
say, 'hey, *look*, there goes Norman!' I want people to
like my poems, I want people to go mad over my
poems . . ."
I decide that this is probably an honest tape
but a bad one
and I no longer
listen.
about 30 minutes and 3 beer cans later
the tape runs its little tail
out. Norman straightens his tie,
gets off his knees and sits
down.

"Jack M. says he's gotta make 8 grand this year or he's
finished."
I try another
cigar.
"I'm having luncheon with Ray
Bradbury, Tuesday."
I don't answer.
"Jesus!"
he suddenly leaps up, runs into my bathroom and
begins vomiting. it continues for some
time.
"I feel better," he says
coming back
in.
"have another drink," I say.
"I'll drive you to your class in
the morning."
"fine," he says, skimming off the top of a beer.
then he looks at me and asks,
"where have you been published
lately?"
I wave my outstretched
palms and shrug.
"Jesus, tough! what made you lose your
inspiration?"
"drink. people. marriage. people.
marriage again. a child. drink.
people. jobs. no jobs. drink and
people."
"my professor would like you to talk to
his class. he won the Lamont Poetry Prize and he
digs you."

"tell your professor to go to hell. tell him
I'm finished."
"you're touchy."
"no, I'm just a flash in the
pan."
we drink and drink. soon he is asleep
on the couch, 250 pounds of him rattling the ceiling
with his poetry.
I go into the bedroom and set the clock for his
10 o'clock English class. the drink goes down
better now, but climbing into bed
I think, where do these bastards come from and
what has happened to everybody? truly, I
am losing it.
the light is out
and then a burglar alarm
somewhere nearby
sifts through his
snoring. very apt, I think,
most apt
for a very wasted night
in December
1965 or
any other time at
all.

another poem about a drunk and then I'll let you go

"man," he said, sitting on the steps.
"your car sure needs a wash and wax.
I can do it for 5 bucks.
I got the wax, I got the rags, I got everything
I need."

I gave him the 5 and went upstairs.
when I came down 4 hours later
he was sitting on the steps, drunk.
he offered me a can of beer.
he said he was going to do the car
the next day.

the next day he was drunk again and
I loaned him a dollar for a bottle of
wine. his name was Mike.
a World War II veteran.
his wife worked as a nurse.

the following day I came down and he was sitting
on the steps. he said,
"you know, I been sitting here looking at your car
wondering how to do it best.
I wanna do it real good."

the next day Mike said it looked like rain
and it sure as hell wouldn't make any sense
to wash and wax a car when it was gonna rain.

the next day it looked like rain again.
and the next.

then I didn't see him anymore.
I saw his wife and she said,
"they took Mike to the hospital,
he's all swelled up, they say it's from
drinking."
"listen," I told her, "he said he was going to wax my
car. I gave him 5 dollars to wax my
car."

I was sitting in their kitchen
drinking with his wife
when the phone rang.
she handed the phone to me.
it was Mike. "listen," he said, "come on down and
get me. I can't stand this
place."

when I got there
they wouldn't give him his clothes
so Mike walked to the elevator in his hospital
gown.
we got on and there was a kid in the
elevator eating a Popsicle.
"nobody's allowed to leave here in a gown,"
he said.

"you drive this thing, kid," I said,
"we'll worry about the gown."

I stopped at the liquor store for 2 six-packs
then drove home. I drank with Mike and his wife until

11 p.m.
then went upstairs.

"where's Mike?" I asked his wife 3 days
later.

"Mike died," she said, "he's gone."

"I'm sorry," I said. "I'm very sorry."

it rained for a week after that and I
figured the only way I'd get that 5 back
was to go to bed with his wife
but you know
she moved out a couple of days
later
and an old guy with white hair
moved in there.
he was blind in one eye and
played the French horn.
there was no way I wanted to make it
with him.

so I had to wash and wax my own car.

dead dog

Bartkowski completes a 58-yard touchdown pass
to beat the Packers in the final minute.
I hear it on the radio
it's Sunday and I'm on the way to the track
I should make the third race.

the Falcons hold on to win and that's good.
I switch off the radio.
then where the Harbor Freeway branches onto
the Pasadena
I see a dog up on the ramp
he's a big one and he's limp
but he's still breathing.
his head is crushed.

people who have dogs in their cars
and let them hang out the window
when those dogs fall out on the freeway
often they just keep driving.

I know how to enter the tunnel.
you take the far right lane while
the other lanes back up on the left.
I glide on through.

when I come out of the tunnel
I slide back into the fast lane.

those sons-of-bitches and their dead
dogs.

I get to the track at 1:20 p.m.
take preferred parking
find a vacant spot at F-5
lock it up
and as I'm walking between cars
I see two men who
have broken into a car.
they are taking out the radio,
the stereo and the speakers.
they see me and I see them.

"don't say *nothin'*, man!
if you do, remember we'll see you
again some day!"

I go inside the track
it's four minutes to post
third race coming up
the crowd has bet Shameen
with Delahousseye riding
down from 4 to 2 to 1.
Song for Two has a line of 2
and reads 3.
I rate the horses even
bet 10-win on Song for Two.

Song for Two wins the photo
the Shoe can still ride
and I'm $31 ahead.

those sons-of-bitches and their dead
dogs.

I lose the 4th, 5th and 6th races.
in the 7th they bet Back'n Time down
to 3-to-5 off a 99 speed rating
6 furlongs down at Del Mar
but the colt is 3 years old
going against older horses
and has never gone a mile.
I can see it turning into the stretch
with a four-length lead and getting beat
at the wire
by something.
but who will do it?
there are 6 other horses.

I put $50 place on Back'n Time
and watch the race.
the colt has four lengths coming into
the stretch
then Don F.
the longest shot on the board
begins to close
and it's tight at the wire.

they hang the photo
we wait
then they put up Don F.
at 19-to-1.

I get $2.80 place
so I make $20
lose the 8th
then I'm up only $18.

in the 9th
I bet 10-win on Fleet Ruler
and 2-win on Forecast
then leave the track
stand out in the parking lot
listen to the announcer
who is hollering
Forecast is in front
and here comes Fleet Ruler
it's Fleet Ruler and Forecast
at the wire.

it's evidently a photo.
I walk to my car to get out of there
before the crowd.

I have the radio
on the race result station.
I'm still on the Pasadena Freeway
when I hear the result:
it's Forecast
and Forecast paid $90.70
so
the day wasn't quite wasted.

but later
when I pull into the driveway
there's the Manx cat
with his rudimentary tail and
with his tongue hanging out.
he refuses to move for the car.
I get out

pick him up and
throw him in the front seat.
we drive into the garage
together.

we get out
the other two cats are waiting
(lovers of fishheads, dreamers of
birds)
I open the door
and all the cats enter along
with me.

they run into the kitchen
I notice that Dallas and San Diego are now
playing. Danny White is at quarterback for
Dallas.
I always liked Danny White,
he's a gambler.

I might watch a few quarters.
Sunday's a day of rest.
all important things should be forgotten.

I decide to not even feed the cats
for a while.
and Tuesday or Wednesday I'll start working
on my childhood novel
again.

I live in a neighborhood of murder

the roaches spit out rusted
paper clips
and the helicopter circles and circles
smelling for blood
searchlights leering down into our
bathrooms
searching for our two-lid cache under the
mattress.
5 guys in this court have pistols
another a
machete
we are all murderers and
alcoholics
but there are worse in the hotel
across the street;
they sit in the green and white doorway
banal and depraved
waiting to be
institutionalized.

here we each have a dying green plant
on our porch
and when we fight with our women at 3 a.m.
we do so
in hushed tones
as outside on each porch
stands a small dish of food
that is always eaten by morning
we presume
by the
cats.

the bombing of Berlin

the Americans and English would come over, he told me,
there was nothing to stop them,
they had red and blue lights on their planes
and they took their time,
and it was funny, you know,
a bomb would take out an entire block
and leave the block next to it standing,
untouched.
once, after a raid, we heard a piano playing
under the rubble
and there was an old woman under there playing the piano,
the building had collapsed all around her,
buried her there and she was still playing the
piano.
after a while, when the planes came again and again
we wouldn't bother to go underground anymore,
we just stayed wherever we were
on first and second floors and looked up
and watched
the red and blue lights and thought,
goddamn them!
well, he said, picking up his beer with a sigh,
we lost the war, and that's all there is to
that.

all right, Camus

met this guy, somewhere, hell his eyes looked like a madman's
or maybe it was only my reflection there.
well, anyway, he said to me, you read Camus?
we're both in this womanless bar looking
for a piece of ass or some way out through the top of the sky and
it wasn't working—there was just the bartender wondering why he'd
ever gone into the business
and myself, very discouraged with the fact that I had now been trans-
    lated only
into 6 or 7 languages.
the guy kept talking—

The Stranger, you know, the book that depicts our modern society—
about the deadened man who
couldn't cry at his mother's funeral, who
killed an Arab or two without even knowing why—

he kept on and on

and on and on
telling me what a son-of-a-bitch *The Stranger*
was, and I kept thinking maybe he's right—
you know, those awful speeches before the French Academy—
you couldn't tell whether Camus was talking out of the
side of his mouth or
whether he was
serious. he certainly sounded no better then than
the guy next to me at the bar
and we were only looking for
pussy.

it was very sad—
all along *The Stranger* had been my hero
because I thought he'd seen beyond trying
or caring
because it was all such a bore
so senseless—
life a big hole in the ground looking up—
and I was wrong again:
hell, I was *The Stranger* and the book simply hadn't come out the way
it was meant to
be.

quits

they made their first mistake when they
laid the champ
facedown
on the dressing room table—
it was a cancer
scream—

and then he cursed them in poor man's
Italian and said
turn me over turn me over turn me over you assholes
turn me over,
and they did
and he said,
>   he broke every rib on my left side
>   he's a murderer, he's not a fighter,
and then he
said,
>   look, get me a gun, I'm going to kill that son-of-a-
>   bitch.

take it easy, champ, said his manager, it wasn't for the title, you
still got the title. you can beat him
in the rematch. we ain't signed the contract to
fight Sondelle yet. we'll hold off on
Sondelle and get this guy in the
rematch.

>   I'm not fighting that killer again, said the
champ,
>   they ought to bar that dirty cocksucker from the
>   ring.

look, champ, said his manager, don't be
stupid, we'll get a real big
gate for the next
one, they'll want to see if he can
do it again.

the champ cursed them in Italian and then said,
    you'll never get me in the ring with that
    killer again.

look, champ, he's a bum I tell you, a bum, he's never beat
anyboby before. next time you
dance away, lay off the
drinking and fucking for a
week, he can't
touch you when you're right. he can't beat
shit, champ.

    he beat
    me. I'll never take another beating like that for
    anyone.

you gonna quit, champ? you gonna quit?

    I'll fight anyone but that
    guy.

all right

so, o.k., how about an X-ray of my
ribs? I can't breathe, really, I
feel them poking into my
lung.

they took him out of there and drove him in a low
long black
limousine
to the private hospital where the
X-rays showed
no breaks.

they're lying, screamed the champ, the fucking
idiots are lying! don't you think I
can feel my own bones when they are
broken?

nobody said anything.

Adolf

I have a friend who has a
scrapbook devoted to Hitler
and his Nazi buddies
and the walls are
covered with old
snapshots of Al Capone
Fatty Arbuckle
Roy Rogers and
many many others.
the walls are limp with rotting glue
and memories, and there are
hidden switches that set off
a frenzy of colored
lights—
each pattern different,
never
the same—
and down in his cellar there are
tons of rain-fattened and rat-
eaten
papers; it's very
dark down there
and there are many
half-finished paintings with
one eye staring up at you
from the floor.
we leave and
go up a
syphilitic staircase and back into
the kitchen where
a hog's head is swimming
in a very large white

pot along with
onions
carrots
potatoes,
one small onion floating in an
empty eye,
and there's his
daughter
2 and one half feet tall
who remembers me
from another
day.
she says some genuine funny things
to us
then walks away into an
upstairs
bedroom
while her father and I sit around
listening to old German
marching songs
and smoking
Picayunes.

the anarchists

one time I began sitting around my place
with some fellows with long dark beards
who were very intense.
many people come to see me but
I usually roust them after a while.
none of them ever bring women,
they hide their women.
I drink beer and listen, but not too
attentively.
but this particular crowd kept coming
back. to me it was mostly beer and
chatter. I noticed that they
usually arrived in a caravan and had
some central yet confused organization.
I kept telling them that I didn't give
a fuck—either about America or about
them. I just kept sitting there and each
morning when I awakened they'd be gone—
and that was best.
finally they stopped coming and a
few months later I wrote a short story
about their political chatter—which,
of course, trashed their idealism.
the story was published somewhere and
about a month later the leader walked
in, sat down and split a six-pack.
"I want to tell you something, Chinaski,
we read that story. we held a council
and took a vote on whether to murder
you or not. you were spared, 6 to 5."
I laughed then, some years ago,
but I no longer laugh. and even

though I paid for most of the beer and
even though
some of you fellows pissed on the
toilet lid, I now appreciate that
extra vote.

perfect white teeth

I finally bought a color tv
and the other night
I hit on this movie
and here's a guy in
Paris
he has no money
but he wears a very good suit
and his necktie is knotted perfectly
and he's neither worried nor drunk
but he's in a café
and all the beautiful women are
in love with him
and somehow he keeps paying his rent
and walking up and down staircases
in very clean shirts
and he advises a few of the girls
that while they can't write poetry
he can
but he doesn't really feel like it
at the moment—
he's looking for Truth instead.
meanwhile he has a perfect haircut
no hangover
no nervous tics around the eyes and perfect
white teeth.

I knew what would happen:
he'd get the poetry, the women and
the Truth.

I popped off the tv set
thinking, you dumb-ass son-of-a-bitch
you deserve
all
three.

4 blocks

I drove my daughter to the school auditorium
where her mother was to meet her
at 5 p.m.
I let her out of the car
and she reached her head back through the window
and kissed me
as she always did.
she was 8. I was 52.
two fat women stood watching us.
I waved goodbye to my daughter
and as she walked to the doorway
one of the fat women asked her,
"wait a minute, who was that man?"
and she answered, "that's my daddy."
then one of the fatsos ran toward me:
"wait a minute, can I get a ride, just 4
blocks?"
"I have a very dirty car," I said.
"I don't mean to intrude," she said,
getting in,
"just follow the road. it's not far."
I followed the road.
"Marina," she said, "is a very nice girl, we
all like Marina."
"yes," I said, "she's a very quiet and
gentle girl."
"yes," she answered, "yes, she is."
"I'm usually very quiet and gentle too,"
I said.
"well," she replied, "I guess if you don't
praise yourself, nobody else will, hahaha!"

"it's quite windy today," I said.

"now," she said, "go two blocks north, then turn
right."

"all right," I said, "I will."

"I hope," she said, "that I'm not taking you too far
out of your way? I hope that I'm not
intruding?"

"have you met Marina's mother?" I asked.

"oh yes," she said, "she's a lovely person, quite a
lovely person."

"are you sure somebody else will?" I asked.

"will what?" she asked.

"praise you if you don't praise yourself," I
replied.

"well," she said, "it's 3 more blocks,
then you take a right."

I ran up 3 blocks and took a
right.

"now," she said, "see that truck with the gate hanging
open?"

"I see it," I said.

"you just park right there by that truck and I'll
get out."

I parked there and she got
out.

"I sure want to thank you," she said,
"and I hope I didn't
intrude."

"I'll see you around," I said,
"take care of yourself."

I drove ahead and took another right
onto a one-way street. the ocean was
down there. there was not a sailboat
in sight. vaguely I wondered about
flying fish
dismissed them as a myth
spun my car around
at the first opportunity
and headed back
to Los Angeles.

you can't force your way through
the eye of the needle

tearing up poems is my
specialty.
on a given night
I will write between 5 and a
dozen
feeling very good about
all of
them.

the next day
in the cold morning
light
I face them
again:
some have
at best
only a decent line or
two.

to rip and basket
these failures
is pure
pleasure.

there are some
days
when all of them
go.

the poem is hardly the
core of our

existence
although
there have been many
poets
who felt that
it
was.

whatever they are,
the gods are not
dumb.
they must laugh
and wonder
at our
fever for
fame.

two kinds of hell

I sat in the same bar for 7 years, from 6 a.m.
until 2 a.m.

sometimes I didn't remember going back
to my room.

it was as if I was sitting on that bar stool
continuously.

I had no money but somehow the drinks kept
coming.
I wasn't the bar clown but rather the
bar fool.
but often a fool can find an even greater
fool to
treat him to drinks.
fortunately,
it was a crowded
place.

but I *had* a point of view: I was waiting for
something extraordinary to
happen.

but as the years drifted past
nothing ever did unless I
caused it:

a broken bar mirror, a fight with a 7-foot
giant, a dalliance with a lesbian,
the ability to call a spade a spade and to

settle arguments that I did not
begin, and etc.

one day I just upped and left.

just like that.

and as I began to drink alone I found my own company
more than satisfactory.

then, as if the gods were annoyed by my peace of
mind, the ladies began knocking at my door.
the gods were sending ladies to the
fool!

the ladies arrived one at a time and when one left
the gods immediately—without allowing me any respite—would send
another.

and each seemed at first to be a fresh miracle, but then everything
that at first seemed wonderful ended up
badly.

my fault, of course, yes, that's what they usually told
me.

the gods just won't let a man drink alone; they are jealous of
simple pleasures; so they send a lady to
knock upon your door.
I remember all those cheap hotels; it was as if all the women
were one; the first delicate rap on the wood and then,
"oh, I heard you playing that *lovely music* on your radio. we're

neighbors. I'm down in 603 but I've never seen you in
the hall before!"

"come on in."

and there went your sanctity.

you also remember the time when
you walked up behind the 7-foot giant and knocked off his
cowboy hat, yelling,
"I'll bet you're too tall to suck your mother's
nipples!"

and somebody in the bar saying, "hey, sir, forget it, he's a mental
case, he's an asshole, he doesn't know what he is
saying!"

"I know EXACTLY what I am saying and I'll say it again,
'I'll bet you were too tall . . .' "

he won the fight but you didn't die, not the way you died inside after
the gods arranged for all those ladies to come knocking at your door.

the fistfight was more fair: he was slow, stupid and even a little
bit frightened and the battle went well enough for you for quite a while,
just like it did at first with those ladies the gods
sent.

the difference being, I decided, I at least had a chance with the
ladies.

my faithful Indian servant

I reached over to turn on
the lights. the lights were already
on. I was in a bad way. "Hudnuck!"
I bawled for my faithful Indian
servant. "kiss my sack," he answered.
in the dim light
I saw him on the couch with
my wife. I stepped outside
and blew my bugle.
3 camels answered my call, and came
running across the yard.
"Hudnuck!" I bawled.
"hold your horses, daddy-o," he answered,
"until I'm finished."
I blew my bugle. nothing happened.
it was full of spit and
tears.
Hudnuck stepped out on the
porch, pulling his zipper closed.
"I want a raise," he said,
"I'm working for nothing."
"and I'm living for nothing, Hud:
don't you realize that
I'm a broken man?"
"don't talk that way," he said,
"you've got a nice wife."
my wife stepped out on the
porch. "what are you having
for breakfast, darling?" she
asked.
"bacon and eggs," I answered.
"not *you*, you *fool*! she snapped.

"t-bone and liver sausage," said
Hudnuck.
"thank you, darling," said my nice
wife, going back into our
nest.
I blew my bugle. a crow answered.
Hudnuck ripped the bugle
from my hand. he wiped it
across the front of my best
shirt. (he was wearing
it.)
he played "Hearts and Flowers"
on the damn thing. the tears
welled up in my eyes.
I decided to give him a
raise. looking over, I saw
him twisting my bugle into
the shape of a cross as he
whistled "It Ain't Gonna
Rain No More."

he had strong, sensitive, beautiful
hands. I looked down at my own.
at first I couldn't find them. then quickly
I took them out of my pockets
and applauded
him.

a plausible finish

there ought to be a place to go
when you can't sleep
or you're tired of getting drunk
and the grass doesn't work anymore,
and I don't mean to go
to hash or cocaine,
I mean a place to go to besides
the death that's waiting
or to a love that doesn't work
anymore.

there ought to be a place to go
when you can't sleep
besides to a tv set or to a movie
or to buy a newspaper
or to read a novel.

it's not having that place to go to
that creates the people now in madhouses
and the suicides.

I suppose what most people do
when there isn't any place to go
is to go to some place or to something
that hardly satisfies them,
and this ritual tends to sandpaper them
down to where they can somehow continue even
without hope.

those faces you see every day on the streets
were not created
entirely without
hope: be kind to them:
like you
they have not
escaped.

another one of my critics

I haven't written a good poem
in weeks. she's 15
and she walks in.
"bastard, when are you going to get
out of bed?"
it's ten minutes to noon
so I get up and walk to the typewriter.
she walks up in a Yankees baseball cap and
stares at me.
"DON'T BUG ME!" I scream. "I AM WRITING!"
"imbecile," she says and walks off.

staring at that sheet of white paper
I begin to think that some of my critics are
right.
she walks into the room again and looks at
me.
"blubbermouth," she says, "hello, blubbermouth."
I ignore her.
she reaches up and tugs at my beard.
"hey, when you gonna take that mask off?
I'm sick of that mask."
then she goes to the bathroom
and with the door open she sits on the pot.
she strains: "urrg, urrg, urrg . . ."
I look over.
"listen, you're supposed to
close the bathroom
door when you do that."
"well, *close* it then, dummy," she says.
I get up and close it.

I know a writer who spent 2 thousand dollars
to have a cork-lined room built for
himself but it still didn't improve his
work. I think I'll take my chances
this way.

fog

worst fog
I ever saw

was driving back from
the beach
with my buddy Desmond
when
it came
in

it was so thick
you
could cut it with
your proverbial
knife.

and we were quite
drunk

we couldn't pull
over because
we were afraid of
hitting cars already parked
at the
curb

but we stopped a
moment and
Desmond climbed up
on the hood
and knelt there

and said, "o.k.,
let's go, I'll
guide you!"

and I started
up and
Desmond yelled,
"SHIT! I CAN'T
SEE ANYTHING!"
and he began
laughing and I
began laughing

I could barely
see his ass
bunched up there on
the hood

and then he
said it
again: "SHIT!
I CAN'T SEE
ANYTHING!"

and we both began
laughing again
harder

a laughter we
couldn't stop

the fog all
around us
as we drove
on

we just kept
driving and
laughing

we slipped through
intersection after
intersection
often hearing
engines and horns
but seeing
nothing
until at one
intersection the
fog lifted a
bit

I could make out
a gas station
a café
there was a
green light

and
Desmond was
missing

I pulled over
and parked in the
gas station and
waited

and there came
Desmond walking up
through the
fog

I hollered and
waved and he saw
me

ran to the car
and got in

we drove on into
L.A.

a week later
he went to
Illinois to see
the wife he
had
split with

and I never
saw him
again.

free?

there's an airline
they offer free champagne
but I've been there
before.

when the stewardess came by
I said, no.

it was warm and
it came right out of the
bottle.

the stewardesses went up and down
pouring refills.

it was a smooth flight
but then it
began:
restroom runs.

lines formed.
the barf bags came
out.

I sat there
listening to the
moaning and the
puking.

when we got to the airport
some were still
going at
it.

some puked as they waited for their
baggage. others puked on the
escalators and in the parking lot.
some puked in their cars while
driving home. some were still puking at
home.

when I got home
I switched on the news
opened a cold beer
and let the bath water
run.

imported punch

they keep bringing fighters up
from Brazil and Argentina
with records like 11–2–1 or
7–4–0
and they're all 27 or 28 years
old
and they put them in with
our boys
with records like
22–0–0,
ages 21 or
22.

the Brazilians and Argentines
fight proudly
and
they hardly lack
guts
but they are built
short and slow
still use boxing
techniques that went out
in the
twenties.
it's more than sad
and I wonder what
these Brazilians and
Argentines think
after they are
bloodied
and then
k.o.'d?

it's just
another dumb fucking flight
back to South America
for them
as they pass their
compatriots
flying North
with no chance
at all.

it was an UNDERWOOD

my poems keep renouncing each
other—
this one says this
and that one says that,
and the other says something else
but I find it humorous
as they battle back and
forth—
angry featherweights, well,
maybe welterweights,
and then I walk into a stationery store—
after all that furious battle—
look at the typewriter ribbons
and can't remember
the name of
the machine.

even my typewriter
renounces itself—

"pardon me," I squeeze by the girl at the
register, "they didn't have
what I wanted."
then I walk across the way
where they do
and buy 6 of those
brews that made
Milwaukee
famous.

the creation coffin

the ability to suffer and endure,
that's nobility, friend.
the ability to suffer and endure
for an idea, a feeling, a way,
that's art, my friend.
the ability to suffer and endure
when love fails,
that's hell, old friend.
nobility, art and hell,
let's talk about art for a while.

destiny is my crippled daughter.
look here, it's difficult,
me against them,
with them.
Kafka, let me in!
Hemingway beware!
Hegel, you're funny!
Cervantes, you mean you wrote that
novel at the age of
80?

great writers are indecent people
they live unfairly
saving the best part for paper.

good human beings save the world
so that bastards like me can keep creating art,
become immortal.
if you read this after I am long dead
it means I made it.

so writers of the world
it's your turn now
to misuse your wife
abuse your children
love thyself
live off the funds of others
dislike all art created before and
during your time,
and dislike or even hate humanity
singly or en masse.

bastards, even if you read this
after I am long dead
forget about me. I
probably wasn't that
good.

the 7 horse

two old guys behind me are talking.
"look at the 7 horse. he's 35-to-1.
how can he be 35-to-1?"

"yeah, he looks good to me too," says
the other old guy.

"let's bet him."

they get up to make their bets.

I've already bet. I've got 40-win
on the 2nd favorite.
I win four days out of five at the
racetrack. it doesn't seem to be
a problem.

I open my newspaper, read the financial
section, get depressed, turn to the front
page looking for robbery, rape, murder.

the two old men are back.
"look, the 7 horse is 40-to-1 now,"
says one of them.

"I can't believe it!" says the
other.

the horses are loaded into the gate, the
flag goes up, the bell rings, they break
out.

it's a mile-and-one-sixteenth, they
take the first turn, go down the backstretch,
circle the last turn, come down the homestretch, get
to the finish line.

the 2nd favorite wins by a neck, pays
$7.80. I make $116.00.

there is silence behind me.
then one of the old men says, "the 7 horse
didn't run at all."

"nope," says the other, "I don't understand
it."

"maybe the jock didn't try," says
his friend.

"that must be it," says
the other.

like most others in the world
they believe that failure
is caused by some factor
besides themselves.

I watch the two old guys as they
bend over their Racing Form
to make a selection in the
next race.

"gee, look at this!" says one of them.
"they got Red Rabbit 10-to-1
on the morning line. he looks better
than the favorite."

"let's bet him," says the other old
guy.

they leave their seats and move gently to the
betting window

the suicide

I had recently buried a woman I lived with
for three years
was between jobs
my teeth rotting in my mouth
(I burned away the pain with aspirin and
beer).

I was sitting on the broken couch
watching evening change into night
when the phone rang.

it was Morrie.

"yes, Morrie?"

"listen, Mark's here. he says he's got to
see you! he says he's going to commit
suicide!"

"put him on . . ."

"no, he can't talk, he's over the
edge!"

I stepped on a passing roach.
"give me your father," I told him.

Bernie took the wire.
"listen, Bernie," I said, "what's this
bullshit about Mark?"

"it's true! he said that if you don't
get over here now he's going to kill himself!
he needs help, Hank!"

"you think he's really going to
do it?"

"I wouldn't kid about a thing like
this!"

"it's a long way to San Bernardino."

"it's only 50 miles! you can make it
in 45 minutes."

"all right, Bernie . . ."

I finished my beer, walked to my
12-year-old car.
it started and I got on the
freeway.

it was a long, drab, stupid ride.

Mark was one of those people who
always insisted that our friendship
was real
no matter how much effort I
exerted to
stay away from him.

I finally pulled up in front of the
house.
I got out of the car, knocked.

Morrie answered the door.
he had a head tic.
when something upset him his
head started jumping.

it was jumping all over in
the doorway.
"Mark's been staying with us,"
he said, "for the last couple of
weeks."

I walked in.

Mark was sitting on the couch
holding a beer.
he smiled at me.
he was dressed in Bernie's old
bathrobe.
he didn't look
as if he was
contemplating
suicide.

"where's your father?" I asked
Morrie.

"he went to sleep. he went to
bed. he isn't feeling
good."

"it's only 7:30."

"he isn't feeling good."

I sat down. there was a fire going
in the fireplace.

"how about a beer?" Morrie asked,
his head jumping.

"sure. where's your mother?"

"she's not home."

Mark cleared his throat. then, in his
quiet voice he began to talk *about
his writing*: he was now into serial killers. he
had written a novel. he had an
agent. he'd been over to see her that
afternoon. she had a swimming pool. they
had had a swim together in her pool. she
was a looker with great connections. she
realized that his writing was exceptional.
she was going to take over his career and
make him famous and . . .

I tuned him out as he went on and on.
he was wearing a silk scarf around his fat
neck.

I finished my beer and Morrie jumped up,
head bobbing, and got me another.

then I heard Mark's voice again. *your
writing reminds me a great deal of my
own!*

Morrie gave me the beer. I took a
good hit and looked into the fire. a
piece of wood cracked in the moment, a
red spark broke off, shot up, fell
back.

it was nice. it was nice and somehow
reassuring.

"I'd like you to read a chapter from my
novel," Mark said. "do you have that blue
folder, Morrie?"

Morrie had it. he placed it carefully on my
lap.
I opened it, went to the first page
and began reading . . .

Mark couldn't write, never could.
I read on, my teeth beginning to ache.
I asked Morrie,

"you got any whiskey?"

Morrie went for it as Mark sat straight
up in Morrie's old bathrobe, waiting
for my words of praise.

I would find a way of letting him down easily
I hoped
without lying.

the whiskey came and I gulped it down
went on reading
drinking
watching the fire.

Morrie's head kept leaping.

why do some individuals never realize how
wearisome they are?
or do they know and simply don't
care?

I read on, hopeless-
ly.

overcast

I went to see my daughter.
she's eleven and had just
taken a bath and she was getting
dressed in the closet so I
wouldn't see her, and her
mother said, "you know, you like
to make this thing about your
women into a great big drama;
you love it, you love them
fighting and screaming over
you, you think it's humorous,
don't you?"

"now, baby . . ." I said.

"some day a woman is going to
put a knife into your heart,
you're going to be killed and
while you're dying you're going
to say, 'you stuck that thing
into me too far!' "

my daughter came out, fully
clothed, and I told her mother
that I'd bring her back in
3 hours.
about 4 miles away we found
a place to eat.
my daughter had a hamburger
sandwich and milk.
I had fried shrimp with
soup, fries, plus coffee.

we ate, I tipped the waitress,
I paid the cashier, then
we went out and got into my
car. it was a dark day, low
clouds, you couldn't see any
sun. "your mother," I told her
as we drove off, "is nothing
but a wiseass."

the final word

always in the poem
we fall short.
ah,
to say the final word
you must
kill the fish,
throw away the
head and tail
(especially the eyes)
and eat the rest.

there is this hunger
to drive down the road
looking for it
in a 1998 Cadillac,
trees along the road,
a dung-spotted moon,
and to run it down
and get out and
look at it,
hold it in your hand
and look at it,
examine it
(especially the eyes)
then throw it all away
and
Cadillac off.

fingernails; nostrils; shoelaces

the gas line is leaking, the bird is gone from the
cage, the skyline is dotted with vultures;
Benny finally got off the stuff and Betty now has a job
as a waitress; and
the chimney sweep was quite delicate as he
giggled up through the
soot.
I walked miles through the city and recognized
nothing as a giant claw ate at my
stomach while the inside of my head felt
airy as if I was about to go
mad.
it's not so much that nothing means
anything but more that it keeps meaning
nothing,
there's no release, just gurus and self-
appointed gods and hucksters.
the more people say, the less there is
to say.
even the best books are dry sawdust.
I watch the boxing matches and take copious
notes on futility.
then the gate springs open again
and there are the beautiful silks
and powerful horses riding
against the sky.
such sadness: everything trying to
break through into
blossom.
every day should be a miracle instead
of a machination.
in my hand rests the last bluebird.

the shades roar like lions and the walls
rattle, dance around my
head.
then her eyes look at me, love breaks my
bones and I
laugh.

after receiving a contributor's copy

carping little kettle-fish
griping over your wounds
found in these misprinted pages,
and still looking for sponsors
lovers
mothers
easy fame:
which one of you
did I see through a
frozen Denver restaurant window
eating apple pie?
which one of you
rode to East Hollywood on a bloodhound
hunting your wet nurse?
which one of you then knocked
on my door
wanting to talk about POETRY?

which one of you is vain enough
and miserable enough
and sick enough
to suck an editor's ass?

which one of you goes
to all the lit parties
and reads his stuff to
tapeworms?   .

which one of you thinks
he's Pound, or Shelley
on a blue butterfly?

which one of you
changed my poem to read
the way you THINK
a poem should read?

which one of you mewed in
sick, friendly sentiment
like larvae crawling the
body of my mind?

and this may seem strong
and unfair,
for I say let everyone live
and write
who wants to live and write,
but which one of you
lives with his mother or his aunt,
which one of you first
puts talcum on his butt
and then climbs up on
the cross?

which one of you
(one a university prof
I once chastised
for senseless abstraction)
which one of you now
writes about whores and drinking
and has never been to bed with a woman,
and has never drunk
more than a small brown beer?

and which one of you
writes with a dictionary against his belly
like buggering an unabridged cow?

which one of you grinds his soul
to Bach's organ
like a monkey on a string?

which one of you
hates the wife that feeds you?
not because she's human
but because
she doesn't like your stuff.

which one of you
couldn't hit a baseball?
which one of you
has never been in jail?

which one of you?
   which one of you?
      which one of
         you?

poor night

I think I'm in the first
dry period of my life.

nearing 62
one fears senility and
an end
to the luck.

I slowly drink
two large glasses of wine
and stare
at the white page.

it has always come so
easily.

I have always laughed at
writers who claimed that
creation was
painful.

I change stations
on the radio, pour
another wine.

"papa," she opens the
door, "do you have any
matches?"

"sure," I say and
hand her a couple of
books.

she leaves.

Henry Miller is dead.
Saroyan. Jeffers.
Nelson Algren.

They've all been dead now
for some time.

"papa," she returns,
"this pen I'm using is
terrible. do you have
another pen?"

"sure," I say and
hand her a good
one.

"there is too much smoke
in this room!"

she opens a window.

"you should let some of
the smoke out!"

"you're right,"
I say.

she leaves
and I like her
concern

but then I am alone
with my blank page
again.

a) so then
I wrote this down to
fill in the blank
space.

b) then came the decision
whether to tear it up or
save it.

c) have
I done
the right thing?

you write many poems about death

yes, and here's another one
and later it might even end up in one of my
books.

and
the book will be sitting on a
shelf
waiting for you
long after I am
gone.

think of that:
in a sense I will be speaking again
just to you.

and remember this:
the page you are looking at
now,
I once typed the words
with care
with you in mind
under a yellow
light
with the radio
on.

if you think about death
long enough
I have found
it belongs
it makes sense
just like

this typewriter
this matchbook
this paper clip

and
the next page
and the next poem
after this
one.

four

the wisdom to quit

is all we have

left.

dog

is much admired by Man
because he believes in
the hand which feeds
him. a
perfect
setup. for
13 cents a
day you've got
a hired killer
who thinks
you are
God. a
dog can't tell a Nazi from a
Republican from a Commie from
a Democrat. and, many times,
neither can I.

the hatred for Hemingway

I gave Hemingway's last book
Islands in the Stream
a bad review
while most others gave him
good reviews.
but the hatred for Hemingway
by the unsuccessful writer
especially the female writer
is incomprehensible to me.

this unsuccessful female writer was in a rage.
I had tried to explain why I thought
Hemingway wrote as
he did.

that life-through-death bit, she said,
is not at all unique with
Hemingway. what else is our
whole Western culture about? it's the same story
over and over
again. no news
there!

that's true, I thought, but . . .

shooting lions only meant shooting
himself? she asked. does it? does
it? not when those lions were unarmed and
he was coming at them with a rifle and
didn't even have to
come close. really! poor little Heming-
way.

it's true, I thought, the lions don't carry
rifles.

the Spanish tradition. I can see Goya because he comes
through as real and complete, she said. I can't see
Hemingway as anything but an old Hollywood movie
acted out by . . . what's his name? that Cooper who was a friend
of his—the *High Noon* guy. oh wow!

she doesn't even like his friends,
I thought.

you learn about death by dying
not by looking at it,
she said.

that's true, I thought, but then
how do you write about it?

you say Shakespeare bores you, she said—
the fact is
he knew far more than Hemingway—
Hemingway never got to be more than a
journalist.

taught to write by Gertrude Stein, I thought.

he told you what he saw, she said, but he didn't know
what it *meant*—how things really
relate . . . he never
explained.

that's strange, I thought, that's exactly what I
liked about
him.

you talk a lot of typical
crap, she said.

what a shame, I thought,
she has such long beautiful
legs. well, Goya was all right too,
but you can't go to bed with
Goya.

well, all right, I thought, Hemingway pulled those big fish
out of the sea and endured a few wars
and watched bulls die and shot some
lions;
wrote some great short stories
and gave us 2 or 3
good early
novels;
on his last day
Hemingway waved to
some kids going to school,
they waved back, and he never touched the orange juice
sitting there in front of him;
then he stuck that gun into his mouth like a soda straw
and touched the trigger
and one of America's few immortals
was blood and brain across the walls and
ceiling, and then they all smiled,
they smiled and said,

ah, a fag! ah, a coward!
yes, he took advantage of McAlmon
he took advantage of everybody
and he didn't treat Fitzgerald right
and he typed standing up
and he was once in a mental
hospital,
and Gertie Stein, that friggin'
dyke,
maybe she did
teach him how to
write.

but who convinced him that it was time to die?

you did, you
dirty
fuckers.

looking at the cat's balls

sitting here by the window
sweating beer sweat
mauled by the summer
I am looking at the cat's balls.

it's not my choice.
he sleeps in an old rocker
on the porch
and from there he looks at me
hung to his cat's balls.

there's his tail, damned thing,
hanging out of the
way so I can
view his furry storage tanks but
what can a man think about
while looking at a cat's nuts?
certainly not about the sunken navy after a
great sea battle.
certainly not about a program to save the
poor.
certainly not about a flower market or a dozen
eggs.
certainly not about a broken light switch.

balls iz balls, that's all,
and most certainly that's true about
a cat's balls.
my own are rather soft and mushy and
I'm told by my current lady
quite large:
"you've got big balls, Chinaski!"

but the cat's balls:
I can't figure whether he's hung to them
or whether they're hung to him.
you see, there is this almost nightly battle for
the female
and it doesn't come easy for either of us.

look:
a piece is missing from his left ear.
once I thought one of his eyes had been
clawed out
but when the dried
blood peeled away
a week later
there was his pure
gold-green eye
looking at me.

his entire body is scarred from bites
and the other day,
attempting to pet his head
he yowled and almost bit me—
the skin on his skull
had been split to reveal the bone.
it certainly doesn't come easy for any of us,
poor fellow.

he sleeps
now dreaming
what?
a fat mockingbird in his mouth?
or surrounded by female cats in heat?

he dreams his daydreams
and we'll find out
tonight.

good luck, old fellow,
it doesn't come easy,
hung to our balls we are, that's it,
we're captive to our balls,
and I should use a little restraint myself
when it comes to the ladies.
meanwhile I will
watch their eyes and lead with the left jab
and run like hell
when it just isn't any use
anymore.

contributors' notes

WENDELL THOMAS teaches creative writing every summer at Ohio State University. His recent credits include *Lick*, *Out of Sight*, *Entrails* and many other important small mags.

RICHARD KWINT recently moved from South Carolina to Delaware. He is now divorced and is currently working on several one-act plays.

TALBERT HAYMAN has appeared in over 23 anthologies. His 3rd chapbook of poems *Winter Driven Light of Night* will be published by the Bogbelly Press later this fall. He is on the faculty of Princeton Day School in N.J.

WILLIAM PREWIT has been widely published in the little mags. He lives with his aunt, his daughter (Margery-Jean), his wife and his tomcat (Kenyon) in upper New Jersey.

BLANDING EDWARDS founded the little magazine *Roll Them Bones*.

PATRICIA BURNS is a genius. She teaches at Princeton Day School in N.J.

ALBERT STICHWORT has worked as a dishwasher, veterinarian, lumberjack, hotwalker, stevedore, motorcycle policeman; he studied under Charles Olson and once fought four rounds with Joe Louis. He has lived in Paris, Munich, London, Arabia and Africa. He is presently studying Creative Writing at the University of Southern California.

NICK DIVIOGONNI rides her horse every day and teaches summer classes at Montclair State Jr. College in N.J.

PETER PARKS teaches at Princeton Day School in N.J.

MARCEL RYAN once shaved the hair off the balls of Jean-Paul Sartre.

PETER FALKENBERG is the father of 3 children and has worked as a janitor, payroll clerk and as an attendant in a mental hospital.

VICTOR BENNETT has appeared in the *North American Review, Southern Poetry Review, Quixote, Meatball, Wormwood Review, Hearse, Harper's, Evergreen Review, Ramparts, Avant Garde, Northern Poetry Review, The Smith, The New York Times, Chelsea, The New York Quarterly, Atom Mind, Cottonwood Review, Antioch Review, Beloit Quarterly, Sun* and *Mummy*. He committed suicide November 9, 1972.

DARNBY TEMPLE is part owner of a Turkish bath.

STUART BELHAM masturbates 4 times a day.

HARLEY GABRIEL plans to teach English next year at Princeton Day School in N.J.

WILLIAM COSTWICK was born in 1900 in Yokohama, Japan.

MASH EDWARDS once raped a girl riding a bicycle. He has studied under Wendell Thomas, Albert Stichwort, Tyrone Douglas, Abbot Boyd, Peter Parks and many others. His main influence is Dame Edith Sitwell.

TANNER GROSHAWK is wanted for the murder of 4 high school students.

SASSON VILLON is a former friend of Victor Mature. He teaches at Princeton Day School in N.J.

VICTOR WALTER writes his poems with flaming fencing swords on the throats of vultures and hates television.

STUART BELHAM'S wife, Tina, masturbates 4 times a day.

CARSON CRASWELL asks for no contributor's note.

TALBOT DIGGINS douses his 4-year-old daughter in scalding water once or twice a week. He edits the poetry newsletter *The Invisible Heart*.

PARKER BRIGGS is presently an "A" student at Montclair State Jr. College in N.J.

on beer cans and sugar cartons

the ox, me,
I am cold tonight
this morning
4 a.m.
down to one can of beer and 2
cigars;
woman and child moving out
Wednesday;
the radio plays a Scottish air and
the old stove muffs out
gas, gas, gas,

if I could only sleep.
I can't seem to sleep.

death doesn't always arrive like a bomb
or a fat whore
sometimes death crawls inch-by-inch
like a tiny spider crawling on your belly
while you
sleep.

this is not news to you,
I know that.

my skeleton hands pray tonight
pray for something
I don't know
what.

my hands hold this cigar
over my emptied
dream.

I am
kind of like a dirty joke
told too often told too late
when people can no longer
laugh.

there is a box on the table.
I read its label, it says:
sugar measurements: 1 lb. powdered equals
4 and ¾ cups sifted; 1 lb. granulated equals
2 and ½ cups, etc.

now, *there's* a new world! I sit and leer at the box,
forgetting everything:
General Grant
pea soup
etc.

the ox, me, I am cold tonight.
tomorrow I will go to the grocery store and get empty cartons
so they can pack up their
stuff. the woman saves all kinds of letters, ribbons,
photographs. the little girl, of course, has her
little girl toys.

I need more to read. I read my beer can. it says:
brewed of pure Rocky Mountain spring water

which turns to piss; brewed of flesh which
turns into a meal for maggots;
brewed of love which turns to nothing; my land and
your land; my grave and your grave; a taste of
honey; a night's dream of gold; I came this way for
a while and then I left: brewed, screwed,
borrowed, loaned and lied to in the name of
Life.

I drink that beer.

I paid for
it.

it is now 5:30 a.m. and many people have fucked and
slept and are now coming up out of their small dreams as
the man on the radio asks me if I want to borrow money on
my home.

I can sleep on that. I can sleep thinking
maybe the next time there are riots in the streets
maybe they'll let me join them
even though my skin is the wrong shade
and while they are fighting for Cadillacs and
color tvs
I'll be fighting for something else—
just what
right now
isn't clear to
me.

but maybe when I awaken it will all be clear.

right now
it's stub out the cigar
wait for the grocery store to open and
change these dirty
shorts.

pay your rent or get out

somewhere the dead princess
    lies with a new lover;
I have only a few empty packs of
    fags left
fished back out of nets of yearning
    but everything is fine
except the color and demeanor
    of the wasp,
the wax too red
and a note from the woman
    on the hill
who buys my paintings:
"wondering about you. call
    me. love, R.,"
and another note under the
    door:
"pay your rent or get out."
the heater is on and
there's a pot of pure ground
    pepper facing me,
and typewriter paper
to fill with poems;
everything is fine,
sidewalks echo the click of
    heels,
engines start,
and I must wash these bloody
    diseased coffee cups;
and I ask myself, how are you today, my
    friend?
how's it going? disappointed?
    unhappy?

me? it's tough. tough as a
    good poem,
but I feel all right,
    and really,
essentially, pretty soon I am
    going to eat
either hash or stew, something
    out of a can.
I also may lift weights and I
    hope
I keep feeling o.k., although my
    radio is fuzzy
and speaks of silly things like
    good jet service;
it is now 7:30, and this is the
    way men
live and die: not Eliot's way
    but
my way, our way,
quietly as a folded wing,
hate burned out like a tube;
the drapes are coming down
    torn by time
and there is a knife to my left that
    couldn't even cut an onion
but I don't have any onions to
    cut, and
I hope you are feeling
o.k. too.

note on a door knocker

yeah? I said, is that
so?
yes, he said, she lives in
Malibu, I'm going to see her
tonight.
ah, I said, has it been a
long-term relationship?
hell no, he said, I'm not a
masochist.

he fingered his gold chain
and talked about
poetry. he talked about poetry
for an
hour.

I'm not a masochist either, I said,
so will you get
the hell out of
here?

he left. but I knew he'd be
back.

he talked about
poetry. I wrote
it.

he couldn't understand
that it and we
were not
alike.

the American Flag Shirt

now more and more
all these people running around
wearing the American Flag Shirt
and it was more or less once assumed
(I think but I'm not sure)
that wearing an A.F.S. meant to
say you were pissing on
it
but now
they keep making them
and everybody keeps buying them
and wearing them
and the faces are just like
the American Flag Shirt—
this one has this face and that shirt
that one has that shirt and this face—
and somebody's spending money
and somebody's making money
and as the patriots become
more and more fashionable
it'll be nice
when everybody looks around
and finds that they are all patriots now
and therefore
who is there left to
persecute
except their
children?

age

the decency of sweating in a rocker
is reserved for old generals or ancient
statesmen as afternoons ripe with young
girls who have nothing to do but laugh and
walk by.

for me
when the fingers go the brain will go,
there will be nothing to lift the
glass and I will sit around thinking of
white nightgowns and hookers
and blocks of night with mice for eyes.

when the fingers fail the cup I have
failed
and the soul
in an old brown bag
will say goodbye
like hedges say goodbye
like cannons sit in parks wondering what
next.

the dogs bark knives

jesus christ the dogs bark knives
and on the elevators
tinkertoy men
decide my life and my death;
the falcons are cross-eyed
and there is nothing to save;
let us know the impossible
let us know that strong men die in packs,
let us know that love is bought and kept
like a pet dog—a dog that barks knives
or a dog that barks love;
let us know that living out a life
among billions of idiots with molecule feelings
is an art in itself;
let us know mornings and nights and
perfidy;
let us be gone with the swallow
let us lynch the last hope
let us find the graveyard of elephants
and the graveyard of the mad;
let those who sing songs of their own
let them sing to the idiots and the liars
and the planners of strategies
in a game too dull for children;
there is only one way to live
and that is alone,
and only one way to die, and that the same;
I've heard the marching of their armies
all these years;
how tiresome—
what they want and what they've won;
how tiresome that they are my masters

and will probably follow me into death
bringing more death to death;
the whole way is hollow—
I touch a small ring on my finger
and breathe the beaten
air.

the hog in the hedge

you know, driving through this town or any town
walking through this town or any town I see
people with nostrils, fingers, feet,
eyes, mouths, ears, chins, eyebrows and so forth.
I go into a café, sit down and order breakfast,
look around and I am conscious of skulls and skele-
tons as I watch a man stick
a piece of bacon into his mouth and die a little
and I don't like to contemplate death because
there *might* be someplace else we have to go later on
and I've had enough trouble right here just being right here
but
maybe it's the fault of all the snakes in glass cages,
they can't move, breathe or kill and they
ought to let them out and they ought to empty the
jails too just as soon as I get my luger in order and
my dogs unleashed.

the buildings are all poorly constructed and the human
body is too; I sometimes watch dancers leaping
about and I think, that's ugly and awkward,
the human body is constructed wrong, it's ungainly and
stupid . . . compared to what? compared to the cactus
and the leopard. well,
my women have always said, "you're so *negative*!"
and I've looked at them and replied, "I find real-
ity negative." compared to what? *unreality.*
yet for all that I have had more joy than any of
them, they were *positive* and depressed, and I am *negative*
and happy. well,

it all could be the fault of firemen sitting around waiting
for a fire, it could be the fault of some guy in Moscow raping
a 6-year-old girl, or it could be because fog is no
longer fog the way it used to be—fresh, wet, cooling,
but everything's hurting now. they found some guy playing
football at U.C.L.A. who couldn't read or write
but Christ he had strength, what a body, he might have
slipped by but he got upset and murdered his drug
dealer and they found out after all that he wasn't
much of a college boy, just kind of a kept goldfish
which reminds me

hardly anybody keeps goldfish anymore; you know when
I was a kid, one household out of 3 had goldfish.
what happened to that? some even had
goldfish ponds in the backyard with slimy moss and
dozens of goldfish, small, medium, large,
they lived on bread crumbs and some of those fuckers got
so fat and stupid they just rose to the top and flattened
out, one eye to the sun, quits, like a bad message
from God, but people also quit when they shouldn't.
once there

was a prizefighter, got $5 million for a championship fight,
the Macho Man, had never been defeated but he ran into
a guy who could handle him and after a few rounds he
turned his back and said,
"no mas."
you'd figure for $5 million a man could stand a little
pain, I've watched men have their entire lives destroyed for
55 cents an hour or less.
well,

maybe it's the masonry or maybe it's the water pump, or maybe it's the
hog in the hedge, or maybe it's the end of luck. angels are flying
low tonight with burning wings, your mother is the victim of
her ordinary nightmares as 40 faucets drip, the cat has
leukemia, there are only 245 days left until Christmas, and my dental
technician hates me.
so now

I wake up with a stiff neck instead of a stiff
dick and
you

can always reach me here in
east Hollywood but
please please please
don't
try.

I never bring my wife

I park, get out, lock the car, it's a perfect day, warm
and easy, I feel all right, I begin walking toward the
entrance and a little fat guy joins me. he walks at my side.
I don't know where he came from.
"hi," he says, "how you doing?"
"o.k.," I say.
he says, "I guess you don't remember me. you've seen me
maybe two or three times."
"maybe so," I say, "I'm at the track every day."
"I come maybe three or four times a month," he says.
"with your wife?" I ask.
"oh no," he says, "I never bring my wife."
"who do you like in the first?" he asks.
I tell him that I haven't bought my Racing Form yet.
we walk along and I walk faster. he struggles to keep up.

"where do you sit?" he asks.
I tell him that I sit in different places.

"that goddamned Gilligan," he says, "is the worst
jock here. I lost a bundle on him the other day. why
do they use him?"
I tell him that Whittingham and Longden think he's all
right.
"sure, they're friends," he answers. "I know something about
Gilligan. want to hear it?"
I tell him to forget it.

we are nearing the newspaper stand near the entrance
and I slant off toward it as if I was going to buy
a paper.
"good luck," I tell him and drift off.

he appears startled, his eyes look shocked, he reminds me
of a woman who feels secure only when somebody's thumb is
up her ass.
he looks around, spots a gray-haired old man with a
limp, rushes up, catches stride with the old guy and begins
talking to him.

I pay my way in, find a seat far from everybody, sit down.
I have seven or eight good quiet minutes, then I hear a
movement: a young man has seated himself near me, not next
to me but one seat away although there are hundreds of
empty seats.
another Mickey Mouse, I think. why do they always find
me?
I keep working at my figures.
then I hear his voice: "Blue Baron will take the
feature."
I make a note to scratch that dog and I look up and
it seems that his remark was directed to me: there's
nobody else within fifty yards.
I see his face.
he has a face women would love: utterly bland and
blank.
he has remained almost untouched by circumstance, he's
a miracle of zero.
I gaze upon him, enchanted.
it's like looking at a lake of milk
never rippled by even a pebble.

I look back down at my Form.

"who do you like?" he asked.

"sir," I tell him, "I prefer not to talk."

he looks at me from behind his perfectly trimmed black
mustache, there is not one hair out of place;
I've tried mustaches; I've never cared enough for mirrors
to keep a mustache looking that unnatural.

he says, "I've heard about you. you don't like to talk
to anybody."

I get up, take my papers, walk three rows down and sixteen
seats over. I go to my last resort, take out my
red rubber earplugs, jam them in.
being my brother's keeper would only narrow me down to a
brick-walled place
where everything is the same.

I feel for the lonely, I sense their need, but I also feel
that the lonely are for one another and that they should
find each other and leave me alone.

so, plugs in, I miss the flag-raising ceremony, being deep
into the Form.

I would like to be human
if only they would let me.

going to the track is like going anywhere else except,
generally speaking,
there are more lonely people there, which doesn't help.
they have a right to be there and I have a right to be there.
this is a democracy and we are all part of one
unhappy family.

an interview at 70

the interviewer leans toward
me, "some say that you are not
as wild as you used to
be."
"well," I say, "I can't keep on
forever writing poems about
spilling beer into the laps of
whores.
a man matures and moves on to other
things."

"but some still want the same
old Chinaski!"

"and that's just what they've
got," I say.

"tell us about the
racetrack," he suggests.

"there's nothing to
tell."

"you have to wait
until he gets mellow
until after midnight
to hear the really good
stuff,"
says my wife.

the interviewer is not
used to waiting.
he stares at his
notes.
he wants some
grand statements, some
grand conclusions,
something grand to
happen now.
he is confused by his
misconceptions and
preconceptions.

and the worst thing
about him?

he's not
wild
enough.

2 views

my friend says, how can you write so many poems
from that window? I write from the womb,
he tells me. the dark thing of pain,
the featherpoint of pain.

well, this is very impressive
only I know that we both receive a good many
rejections, smoke a great many cigarettes,
drink too much and attempt to steal each other's
women, which is not poetry at all.

and he reads me his poems
he always reads me his poem
and I listen and do not say too much,
I look out of the window,
and there is the same street
my street
my drunken, rained-on, sunned-on,
childrened-on street,
and at night I watch this street
sometimes
when it thinks I am not looking,
the 1 or 2 cars moving quietly,
the same old man, still alive, on his
nightly walk,
the shades of houses down,
love has failed but
hangs on
then lets go.
but now it is daylight and children
who will some day be old men and women
walking through last moments,

these children run around a red car
screaming their good nothings,
then my friend puts down his poem.

well, what do you think? he asks.

try so and so, I name a magazine,
and then oddly
I think of guitars under the sea
trying to play music;
it is sad and good and quiet.
he sees me standing at the window.
what's out there?

look, I say,
and see . . .

he is eleven years younger than I.
he turns away from the window. I need a beer,
I'm out of beer.

I walk to the refrigerator
and the subject is closed.

van Gogh and 9 innings

the battleship nights in Georgia
   when we all
went down.

do you know? there was this Russian who
leaped to music well enough to make you cry
and he went insane
and they put him someplace and fed
   him and
shocked him with electric wires and cold water
   and then
hot water and he wrote books about himself
he couldn't read or
remember.

out at the ball game
in Atlanta
I watched them hurrying, sweating,
and I sat there thinking about the
   Dutchman
(instead of the Russian)
the Dutchman with the toothbrush
   stroke
who never learned to properly mix his
paints and who couldn't make even a
whore love him
and it all ended then
for him and for the whore
and he cut off his ear and continued to
beg for paints
and they write books about him
now

but he's dead and can't read them
and I saw some of his stuff at a
    gallery,
last year—they had it roped off and
guarded so you couldn't touch the
    work.

somebody won that ball game in Atlanta and the
whore
didn't want his
ear.

9 a.m.

blazing as a fort blazes
this first impromptu note—
sunlight—
foul betrayer
breaking through kisses and perfume and nylon,
showing a city of broken teeth
and insane laws,
bringing a ruined alley to the eye,
this diamond in the rough;
and inside my palm
a small sore
berry-red
that even Christ w'd n't ignore
as the ladies pass
shifting their rotted gears
and peppermint fences and spoiled dogs
blazing as
you burn;
9 a.m. sunlight
gives us apples and whores
and now thankfully
I can again remember
when I was young
when I walked in gold
when rivers had mirrors
and there was no end.

lousy day

in the old days
after the races I would often end up with a
high yellow or a crazy white in some motel
room
but now I'm 70 and have to get up four times
each night to piss
and about the only thing that really concerns me is
freeway traffic.
today I dropped $810.00 at the track and when
I tried to enter the freeway a
guy in a red Camaro almost ran me
off the road (red automobiles have always
annoyed me) so I swung after him, rode his
bumper hard, then swung around and we rode side-by-
side.
looking over at him I saw he was a slight young
boy who looked like a cost accountant, so I ran
my window down and screamed at him while
honking, informing him that he was a piece
of subnormal dung but he just continued to stare
straight ahead so I hit the gas and left him
behind and my next thought was, I wonder if I
should tell my wife about this?
and then quickly a voice from somewhere
answered, don't be a sucker, pal, she'll
just turn it into an unflattering joke.

"oh, hahaha! he probably didn't even know
you were there!"

if a man lives for 70 years he learns
one or two things—the first being: don't confide unnecessarily

in your wife.

the second being: others may sometimes

understand you but

none of them will understand you

better than your wife

does.

sadness in the air

here I am alone sitting
like some wimp

listening to Chopin

the night wind blowing in
through the
torn curtains.

won $546 at the track today but
now I'm thinking that
dying is such a strange and
ordinary thing.

I just hope that I'll never need
false teeth before I
go.

. . .

Wm. Holden cracked his head
on a coffee table
while drunk and
bled to death;
stiff and dead for 4 days
before they found him.

I wonder how Chopin went?

things pass away, that's not
news.

here in L.A.
I've seen so many good
Mexican fighters
come and go
climbing through the
ropes
young and glistening with
ambition
and then
vanish.

where do they go?
where are they tonight
as I listen to Chopin?

maybe I'm in a better
business?

I don't think so.

writers go fast
too
they forget how to lead
with a
straight hard sentence

then they teach class
write critical articles
bitch
get stale
vanish.

. . .

Holden slipped on a
throw rug
his head hitting the
nightstand
he had a .22 alcohol
blood count.

myself
I've gone down
many times usually
over a telephone cord.

I hate telephones
anyhow
whenever one rings
I jump.

people ask, "why do you
jump when the telephone
rings?"

if they don't know
you can't tell them.

. . .

it's getting cold.
I go to shut the window.
I do.

Chopin continues.

when you drink alone
like Wm. Holden
sometimes you've got
something on your mind
that you can't tell
anybody.

in many cases it's
better to keep
silent.

we were not put here to
enjoy easy days and
nights

and when the telephone
rings
you too will know that
we're all
in the wrong business

and if you don't know
what that means
you don't feel the
sadness in the air.

the great debate

he sent me his latest book.
I had once liked his writing
very much.

he had been wonderfully crude, simple,
troubled.

now he had learned how to gracefully
arrange his words and thoughts
on paper.

now he taught courses at the
universities.

but I wondered about
what?

his words were now
very pale.

they spread across the page
like a mist
filling it
but saying
very little.

he didn't seem to be the
same man.
where had he gone?

why do
such deaths seem
mysterious?

it's well that
new poets come along
new quarterbacks
new matadors
new dictators
new revolutionaries
new butchers
new pawnbrokers.
because spiritual death arrives
much more quickly and unexpectedly than
physical demise.

I drop his new book
into the wastebasket.
I don't want it
around.

he was now a
successful writer
which meant
that his work
no longer made
anybody
angry
disgusted
or sad.

never made
anybody
laugh

never made
anybody
feel that rush of wonder
while reading
it.

but in a world
where even
the disappearance
of the dinosaur
remains a mystery
we should accept
the mysterious fact of
the vanishing poet.

and when we accept
that
we are simply
making way for
our own final
invisibility.

our deep sleep

I've always been a sucker for the
old ones: Céline, Hemingway, Dreiser,
Sherwood Anderson, e. e. cummings,
Jeffers, Auden, W. C. Williams, Wallace Stevens,
Pound, D. H. Lawrence, Carson
McCullers . . . and some others.

Our current moderns
leave me quite
unsatisfied.
there is neither lean nor
fat in their efforts, no pace,
no gamble, no joy.
it's work reading them, hard
work,
there is much pretense
and even some clever con
behind their productions.

I have no idea what has
happened to the creative
writer since the 1940s.
there has been a half century
of utter pap.
why?
I don't know.
I don't know.

there has been little to
read
for some time now.
I have been able to

read only the newspapers
and the
Racing Form.

all those books printed,
a million books
printed
and nothing to
read.

a half century shot to
shit.

we deserve nothing
and that's what we have
now.

the sorry history of myself

this is a terrible way to live:
surrounded by
the ever-
irascible,
coldhearted and
nearly mad.

but my early experiences were
quite similar.

I should be adjusted to it
all by now

from my angry boiling
petty father
to

the slew of females
who came later
all consumed by
depression,
useless rage,
screeching and
nonsensical
self-
pity.

happiness and simple joy
for them all seemed to be
simply diseases to be
eradicated.

this history of
myself:
this terrible way to
live.

but I feel I have now snatched
victory
from all the useless
raging black
hysteria.

I have now survived all
that and
they can club me with their
angry lives and
burn me on my
deathbed

but somehow
I have found a lasting
peace
they can never
take
away.

law

look, he told me,
all those little children dying in the trees,
and I said, what?
and he said, look,
and I went to the window
and sure enough, there they were hanging in the trees,
dead and dying,
and I said, what does it mean?
and he said, I don't know but it's been authorized.
the next day when I got up
they had dogs in the trees
dead and hanging and dying,
and I turned to my friend and said,
what does it mean?
and he said, don't worry about it,
it's the way of things, they took a vote,
it was decided,
and the next day it was cats,
I don't see how they caught all those cats so fast
and hung them in the trees
but they did,
and the next day it was horses and that wasn't so good
because many branches broke,
and after bacon and eggs the next day
my friend pulled the pistol on me
over the coffee and said,
let's go,
and we went outside
and there were all these men and women in the
trees, most of them dead or
dying, and he got the rope ready, and I said,
what does it mean? and he said, don't worry,

it's been authorized, it's constitutional, it passed by
majority vote, and he tied my hands behind my back,
then opened the noose.
I don't know who's going to hang me, he said,
when I get done with you. I suppose, finally,
there'll be just one of us left
and he'll have to hang
himself.
suppose he doesn't? I asked.
he has to, he said, it's been authorized.
o, I said, well, let's get on
with it
then.

a great writer

a great writer remains in bed
shades down
doesn't want to see anyone
doesn't want to write anymore
doesn't want to try anymore;
the editors and publishers wonder:
some say he's insane
some say he's dead;
his wife now answers all the mail:
". . . he does not wish to . . ."
and some others even walk up and down
outside his house,
look at the pulled-down
shades;
some even go up and ring the
bell.
nobody answers.
the great writer does not want to be
disturbed. perhaps the great writer is not
in? perhaps the great writer has gone
away?

but they all want to know the truth,
to hear his voice, to be told some good
reason for it all.

if he has a reason
he does not reveal it.
perhaps there isn't any
reason?

strange and disturbing arrangements are
made; his books and paintings are quietly
auctioned off;
no new work has appeared now for
years.

yet his public won't accept his
silence—
if he is dead
they want to know; if he is
insane they want to know; if he has a
reason, please tell us!

they walk past his house
write letters
ring the bell
they cannot understand and will not
accept
the way things are.

I rather like
it.

a gigantic thirst

I've been on antibodies for almost 6 months, baby, to cure a case of
TB, man, leave it to an old guy like me to catch such an old-fashioned
disease, catch it big as a basketball or like a boa constrictor
swallowing a gibbon; so now I'm on antibodies and been told not to
    drink
or smoke for 6 months, and talk about biting iron with your
teeth, I've been drinking and smoking heavily and steadily with the
    best
and the worst of them for over 50 years, yeah,
and the most difficult part, pard, I know too many people who
drink and smoke and they just go right on drinking and smoking in
    front of me like
I'm not aching to crack their skulls and roll them on the floor
or just chase them the hell away out of my sight—a sight which
longs *very much* for anything even microscopically addictive.
the next hardest part is sitting at the typewriter without it,
I mean, that's been my show, my dance, my entertainment, my
raison d'être, yep, mixing smoke and booze with the typer and you've
got a parlay there where the luck rains down night and day and in
    between, and
you hear the phrase "cutting it cold turkey" but I don't think that's
strong enough, it should be "chopping it cold turkey" or "burying the
    turkey
warm," anyhow it hasn't been easy, no no no no no no no no no no,
and when I look at a bottle of beer
it looks like bottled sunlight, a smoke is like the breath of life
and a bottle of red wine looks like the blood of life itself.

for me, it's hard to think or worry about the future: the immediate
present seems too overwhelming and now I sympathize with all those
who fail
to curb their drinking and their smoking
because these last 6 months have been the longest 6 months of my life!

forgive me for boring you with all this but isn't that why you're
here?

eulogies

after death
we exaggerate a person's good qualities,
inflate them.

during life
we are often repulsed by that same person
while talking to them on the telephone
or just being with them in the same room.

and we are often critical of the way they
walk, talk, dress
live
believe

but let them die
then what creatures they
become.

if only at a funeral service
somebody would say,
"what an odious individual
that one was!"

even at my funeral
let there be a bit of truth,
then the good clean
dirt.

a residue

stuck in mid-flight,
wickedly sheared,
dreaming of the
dactylozoid.

turned away,
fashioned to stop
on zero,
flamed out,
hacked at,
demobilized.

where is common
laughter?
simple joy?
where did they
go?

what a vanishing
trick,
that.

even the skies
snarl.
what rancor,
what
bitterness . . .

the cry of the
smothered
heart,
now

remembering
better
times
wild and
wondrous.

now the sad
grim
present

cleaves.

1990 special

year-worn
weary to the bone,
dancing in the dark with the
dark,
the Suicide Kid gone
gray.

ah, the swift summers
over and gone
forever!

is that death
stalking me
now?

no, it's only my cat,
this
time.

passage

and their ships burned, galleon and galley sail,
and they drowned as the clouds came down
like kings from thrones and held them:
servants, slaves, lions, sages, fools, merchants,
murderers; then the kelp, bitumen, alabaster, seashells
held court, and then came the shadows,
dark as walls under a dying sun: and bellicose and
vicious the sea pounded the sinking ships and the
weeds cradled the skulls in disquisition, the
sea kelp held the skulls up and you saw
them then, so odd and free and casual: all the
lonely lovers dead.

a most dark night in April

each man finally trapped and broken
each grave ready
each hawk killed
and love and luck too.

the poems have ended
the throat is dry.

I suppose there's no funeral for this
and no tears
and no reason.

pain's the master
pain is silent.

the throats of my poems
are dry.

sun coming down

no one is sorry I am leaving,
not even I;
but there should be a minstrel
or at least a glass of wine.

it bothers the young most, I think:
an unviolent slow death.
still it makes any man dream;
you wish for an old sailing ship,
the white salt-crusted sail
and the sea shaking out hints of immortality.

sea in the nose
sea in the hair
sea in the marrow, in the eyes
and yes, there in the chest.
will we miss
the love of a woman or music or food
or the gambol of the great mad muscled
horse, kicking clods and destinies
high and away
in just one moment of the sun coming down?

but now it's my turn
and there's no majesty in it
because there was no majesty
before it
and each of us, like worms bitten
    out of apples,
deserves no reprieve.

death enters my mouth
and snakes along my teeth
and I wonder if I am frightened of
this voiceless, unsorrowful dying that is
like the drying of a rose?

CHARLES BUKOWSKI is one of America's best-known contemporary writers of poetry and prose, and, many would claim, its most influential and imitated poet. He was born in Andernach, Germany, to an American soldier father and a German mother in 1920, and brought to the United States at the age of three. He was raised in Los Angeles and lived there for fifty years. He published his first story in 1944 when he was twenty-four and began writing poetry at the age of thirty-five. He died in San Pedro, California, on March 9, 1994, at the age of seventy-three, shortly after completing his last novel, *Pulp* (1994).

During his lifetime he published more than forty-five books of poetry and prose, including the novels *Post Office* (1971), *Factotum* (1975), *Women* (1978), *Ham on Rye* (1982), and *Hollywood* (1989). Among his most recent books are the posthumous editions of *What Matters Most Is How Well You Walk Through the Fire: New Poems* (1999), *Open All Night: New Poems* (2000), *Beerspit Night and Cursing: The Correspondence of Charles Bukowski and Sheri Martinelli, 1960–1967* (2001), *Night Torn Mad with Footsteps: New Poems* (2001), *sifting through the madness for the word, the line, the way: new poems* (2003), *The Flash of Lightning Behind the Mountain* (2004), *Slouching Toward Nirvana* (2005), and *Come On In!* (2006).

All of his books have now been published in translation in more than a dozen languages and his worldwide popularity remains undiminished. In the years to come Ecco will publish additional volumes of previously uncollected poetry and letters.